RHODE TO ROUEN

RHODE TO ROUEN

A NOVELLA

SHREY SAHJWANI

PARTRIDGE
A Penguin Random House Company

To order additional copies of this book, contact
Partridge India
000 800 10062 62
www.partridgepublishing.com/india
orders.india@partridgepublishing.com

For Lorie

PROLOGUE

James Spurlock and Mia Camello shared a lot of their lives with each other. They shared a hot cup of coffee every Sunday morning, they even shared breakfast. They shared Saturday nights, and that became more religious than habitual. As far as Monday through Friday was concerned; they spent it apart from each other. No one knew about their secret relationship. Not even Mia's husband.

During the week Mia Camello was a 36 year old housewife with two step-kids. An 8 year old boy and a girl, aged 10. She always dressed nicely and spoke wisely. You could tell that you were in the presence of an aristocrat the second she walked into a room. She stayed home while her stock-market-tycoon-husband, Bob, went out into the real world to put food on the table. She was the perfect wife. She worked hard. She cleaned up after herself and the rest of her family and she looked stunning with long brown hair, beautiful hazel eyes and the body of a beauty-pageant winner.

The Camello Family lived in Newport, Rhode Island. They had a beautiful white mansion that they called home. Mia loved her family-life. She had beautiful children that were great with academics, a husband that was outrageously rich and a kicking sex-life. Sadly the sex-life didn't have much to do with her husband. Mia had the ruffled, brown haired, brown-eyed James Spurlock to thank for that.

James was the same person during the course of the week as he was when Mia was with him during the weekend. He hadn't a care in the world. Neither did he have a job nor did he have a career. James had done it all in his time. Started off as an artist, then he later went on to become an author. He never had been published, but when asked he'd say that he was working on it. He lived his life by his own rules and he had none. James was everything that Mia wanted to be, but couldn't.

James wanted to change nothing about his life. He didn't have anything that he sought to achieve. No deadlines. All he needed was to open the creative mind that god had gifted him with, and all he needed for that was marijuana. Luckily, he always had some in his possession along with a platoon of other illegal substances. Whenever Mia was around him, even she couldn't help but indulge. A little cocaine here, maybe a little hashish there. Anything in the name of love or, in their case, lust.

The week went by slow for Mia. She had laundry and other such housework to finish. That, and taking care of two growing children and pretending to be happily married. Her husband was expected to come home every weekday at 7:30 PM. His children always flocked to him when his car came to a halt outside. The kids loved their dad. Mia did too, to some extent. She just couldn't wait for the monotony of the week to end. And for Saturday to arrive so that she could be with James. The man she was fucking behind her husband's back.

Saturday was poker night on Bob's yacht. He had a policy which he followed strictly: Guys only. Poker night lasted all of Saturday night and some of Sunday morning. Mia would arrange for the kids to sleepover either at their friends houses or with a member of their family for the weekend, claiming that she deserved a girl's night out too.

James and Mia had a bond. They were great together. They never bothered about what was or wasn't happening in the world they lived in. They had no responsibilities and they had no worries. It was the best relationship either of them had ever been in.

The two of them met at an art gallery three years prior to this day.

It was raining outside, which was the only reason Mia was even in an art gallery. James was selling a few of his paintings there.

Mia was amazed by the colors she saw around her. She stopped at James' painting. It was one of a disfigured old woman, curled up into the fetal position. He painted it all with just one shade of Brown. Mia stood there and stared for hours on end.

"This lady is a good friend of mine." said James to a confused Mia; as he pointed at the woman in the picture.

She was taken by surprise, she put her left hand on her chest to show how taken aback she was by the stalker-like stunt this strange man had pulled on her. She turned around only to find the man that had made her heart skip a beat had thick brown hair and mystical brown eyes. She was staring at a man in an art gallery who was wearing what seemed like his grandfather's jacket over his unwashed jeans. She liked what she saw, and that surprised her.

"I'm sorry; I didn't mean to startle you. My name is James. James Spurlock." He went on to say while holding his hand out to greet her.

She in turn held out her hand and said, "Hi, I'm Mia. What do you know about the woman in the painting?"

"Judging by the looks of things, she's going through a lot of shit right now." He said with a wry smile.

"Is that why the artist has used just Brown?" she asked, cheekily.

He cracked his knuckles and went on to say, "Well, either that or the artist must've been smoking too much pot to know the difference between that and any other color."

She nodded her head and said, "That's a good read. I'd love to smoke some pot with this artist. Maybe then I'll know what he was thinking when he painted this."

"Sure we could hang out together." he said to her curtly as they exchanged phone numbers.

"What about your husband, will he mind?" James asked, concerned.

"My husband?" Mia was confused. She was wondering how he'd found out about that.

He giggled and said, "The ring on your finger. It's a dead giveaway."

She just smiled and said, "Don't you think you've asked far too many questions for one night, James?"

When he didn't reply, she went on to say, "I have one for you; how much for this old lady?"

"That'll be forty dollars and a date on Saturday night." He replied, with a smile on his face.

"I'll take it." she said, while she held out forty dollars towards him.

"So it's a date then?" asked James, with a sense of hope that you could see clearly in his eyes.

"I believe it is." she said.

James lived in a one bedroom studio apartment in one of the cheapest areas of the city. Mia was always used to living in great homes and mansions but surprisingly, she found James' house inviting. They spent the evening doing drugs and munching on microwave popcorn as they went through several old movies. They started the night laughing away, undressing each other in their minds all night long. All it took for the fantasy to become a reality was one sentence.

"Fancy a quickie?" asked James, in between two old horror movies.

"I have all the time in the world, why settle for a quick one?" counter-questioned Mia.

James leaned forward and kissed her passionately. Mia was being impulsive, she tried not to seem desperate but she couldn't hold back much longer. She dropped the sleeves of her floral dress over her shoulders, exposing her dark purple lingerie. James stared in amazement.

"You're well endowed." he said, while he smiled.

"You like my boobs, do you?" giggled Mia.

James went on to say, "I was just trying to be polite. They're perfect."

He then continued kissing her and in turn, she began undoing his khaki trousers.

A few minutes into foreplay, Mia couldn't wait any longer.

"I want to see all of you." she said, with a thirst for lust in her voice.

"Patience, my dear. It'll take you a long way." he said, with emphasis on the word 'long'

She giggled as he lowered her completely onto the couch. He then began undressing her. Her hips were buckling. She was ready; James knew that and used it to his advantage.

He lowered his head towards her neck and planted several soft kisses, after which he kissed his way down to her abdomen. Mia was squirming now; she felt the shivers run down her spine.

"I must tell you, you have a very skillful tongue." She said between gasps.

James used his skilled tongue to do more than just talk dirty to her. This proved it to her. Several times he brought her close to climax and stopped to kiss her. It drove her crazy but she loved every minute of it.

"Just fuck me already!" she said, in eagerness.

And 'fuck her' he did.

Every Saturday night that followed was the same story:

The husband would leave for his poker-night, her kids would be tucked in elsewhere and Mia would fuck James at his house.

Everything was happening so fast, and years passed by in a matter of seconds.

No sooner did she know it, than she was falling in love with him.

What made things worse, was that he was already in love with her.

CHAPTER 1

RHODE

"I wish life was like a bed of roses." said she.

"In that case; what do you intend to do with the thorns?" he retorted.

———◆———

Sunday: it was the day when every person in the world would take a break from it all. Just spend time alone, be with family and friends and what not. Not James and Mia. That was the last few hours of each other that they had. Once the sun was looming directly overhead; Mia would be thrown out of her fairy tale world and into the real one. Her husband would be returning home from his long night of throwing plastic chips on the table and her children would be home from their grandparent's house.

Mia was wearing a white shirt that had turned grey with time, use and abuse. It was James'.

She was pouring coffee into two cups. She always prepared coffee in the morning. She knew how much James loved his caffeine; one of his many vices.

His house was a shabby, one room apartment. The bed needed to be pulled out of the wall. His floors were always stained by alcohol, food and other such things.

The living room was part of the kitchen. Complete with a stove, fridge and couch.

"Good morning, honey." Mia said as she handed the cup out to him.

"Morning babe." he said as he pecked her lips.

The two of them made their way through the kitchen-cum-living-room and reclined on the couch.

"I hate this part of the day." She complained.

"The saying goodbye part?" he asked.

"I wouldn't call it goodbye." She paused as she stood up and sat on his lap. "It's just us parting until we meet again." She went on to say while planting a passionate kiss on his lips.

"Now, that you put it that way." He smirked.

They kissed for a few minutes and she stood up waved goodbye and walked out the door.

James sat still on his couch, picked up one of the several joints he had made the night before and lit it.

He sat there sipping on coffee and smoking marijuana. He was content. His life was exactly what he wanted it to be; empty with a side of Mia.

Mia made her way home; she sorted out her dress and fumbled in her purse, hoping that she'd find her keys somewhere.

When she couldn't find it; she said out loud, "Where the fuck did I put those keys?" The door in front of her opened and she was taken by surprise.

"Hi honey." said a joyful Bob, "Lose the keys again?"

"Hey honey! You're home already? How was poker night?" she asked as she made her way into the mansion.

He led her to den that served as an office and a library, one of the many spare rooms the family had.

"It was great honey." He paused and went on to say, the happiness in his eyes very easily visible, "Jim had a full house and I flopped a four of a kind. Queens at that! I took that poor bastard to the cleaners!" Mia faked a smile. She didn't understand a word that had just come out of Bob's mouth. "That's great, honey." she said.

"Great? It's fucking fantastic! Do you have any idea how rare a hand like that is?" Bob was behaving like a child.

"No I don't know!" said Mia, curtly.

"Well, it's fucking huge!" said Bob, just as curtly.

"Would you mind your fucking tongue? The kids are running around here somewhere." she said, angrily.

"So it's alright when you say it, but it's not when I do? That's a fucking double-standard." Bob was getting annoyed.

"What has gotten into you?" Mia asked, with tears in her eyes.

"What has gotten into ME?" Bob said, puzzled. He then went on to say, "What has gotten into YOU? I'm not the one that asked about your night and didn't give a shit when the question was answered."

"I was just being polite, asshole! I don't give a shit about your friends or your four of a kind queens. I know you can't satisfy even one of those queens!" said Mia as she barged out of the room.

"Great! Always dig that up, you bitch!" Bob yelled, in despair.

He sat down on the chair beside him, held his forehead and started crying.

Meanwhile Mia sat in her room, regretting ever marrying the man she had just had a fight with.

Bob walked into the room that Mia was in. It was a lavishly furnished master-bedroom. The décor was classy and the ambience was sophisticated. It was the bedroom of Mia's dreams. But she had a different vision of the man who she'd be sharing the bed with.

"Honey, why are we fighting so much?" Bob asked, still crying like a little girl.

"I don't know. I'm tired and frustrated.", you could tell there were many things on her mind when she said that.

"Yeah, you always are." he replied.

She said nothing. Bob took that as his cue and went on to say, "It's not like I want things to be this way, baby." By this point, he was weeping.

Mia was feeling horrible about herself. She knew that Bob loved her like no one else would. She knew that James and she weren't exclusive. James wasn't a long-term prospect. Bob was. She had been married to the man for 5 years.

"Honey, I don't know what to say." she said, as she wiped his tears.

"I know you've been feeling all sorts of hell right now. I've been feeling that way too." he said, while trying to hold the tears back.

Mia was starting to sympathize with him. She loved Bob; that she was sure of. What she wasn't sure of was whether or not she was IN love with him.

"Honey, you know I love you, right?" asked a saddened Bob.

"Yes, and I love you." Mia replied.

"Should we give this another shot?" asked Bob.

Mia smiled, pulled him closer to her and kissed him. They were on the verge of dropping their pants. Just then, Alison; their daughter, walked in and said, "Daddy . . . I can't sleep."

The couple lookbed at each other and shared a laugh about the matter. Bob then went on to say, "Come sleep in between us, honey." Alison smiled and obliged.

Bob was laying there thinking, *"This is the perfect family."*

Whereas Mia was thinking, *"I wonder what James is doing right now."*

———————◆———————

The night passed by quickly. James woke up on the cold floor of his apartment, by the sound of someone knocking profusely on his door.

He stood up; naked, if not for his boxer shorts, and dragged himself to the door. He stared through the blurry peep-hole and saw what looked like a blonde woman.

"Oh shit. What does she want?" he said to himself, softly as he opened the door.

"Hello Jennifer." said James

Jennifer was one of James' ex-girlfriends. She never got over James, and that was mostly his fault. He never did let her go completely. When he was lonely and had nothing better to do; he'd call her and then they'd have sex until the sun came up. That was before Mia came into his life. After that, Jennifer was forced to come to James' apartment unannounced to see him.

Jennifer smiled at him and pounced on him and kissed him passionately.

He picked her up and took her to the couch, while still kissing her. He then dropped her on it and set his body above hers. The kiss, now prolonged, sent a horde of chills down Jennifer's spine, and had a similar effect on James' groin.

He took her top off and she in return strummed her hand down his chest and reached for his crotch. "Blow?" she asked.

"I don't see why I should stop you." said James.

"Where is it?" she asked.

"Where is what?" asked James, puzzled.

"The blow?" asked Jennifer, innocently.

"Oh!" exclaimed James, "You meant cocaine . . ." James was embarrassed.

He got off her, went into the room and got out the white powdery substance in a see-through plastic bag.

He dropped it on the table in front of her.

"Got a credit card?" she asked.

James shrugged and said, "I would, if I had any money."

She looked around and saw a key on the couch. She picked it up and poured some powder on the table as she began filing it into one line.

Jennifer pulled out a metallic stem-like item from her purse.

"Nice coke straw." James said, as he watched her snort the cocaine.

"Want a hit?" she asked, politely.

James smirked and made a line for himself with the key. Just as he was about to snort the drugs he heard the entrance to his apartment open.

The only other person that had the key to his apartment was Mia. She walked into the room and found James with the keys to her house in his hand, a coke straw placed in his nose and a topless woman by his side.

She walked towards him with tears in her eyes. Neither of them said a word to each other for several seconds. Just then the topless woman stood up and put her hand out to Mia and said, "Hi, I'm Jennifer." while trying to cut out the tension.

Mia looked over at James disdainfully and snatched her keys out of his hand and walked out of the apartment, not forgetting to slam the door shut behind her.

James snorted the cocaine and sat back onto the couch.

"What's the matter?" asked Jennifer, while stroking James' chest.

"Get your shit and go!" yelled James.

"What the fuck has gotten into you?" asked Jennifer.

"Just leave." He said.

She put on her top and started to walk out furiously. Just as she was about to walk out the door she asked, "Who was that woman?"

"None of your fucking business!" yelled a frustrated James.

Jennifer didn't say a word as she stormed out of his apartment and slammed the door shut.

James sat there motionless for a while. He knew about the old saying that went, "Hell hath no fury like a woman scorned." He wondered which proverb would be appropriate for two scorned women. He sat there thinking to himself, "Thank god drugs don't have emotions; they would've slammed the door on me a long time ago."

CHAPTER 2

IN YOUR ABSINTHE

"I've broken everything in this house . . . My family, my husband's heart and even some furniture. There's just one thing I have to say to you . . . I'll never ever break you." said Mia; to a bottle of alcohol.

———— •◆• ————

Mia went through the week frustrated. It seemed as though everything in her life was going in the wrong direction. She didn't want to meet James again after what she had witnessed. James had sent her over a dozen emails and messages on her cell phone. She chose not to reply to any of them.

Her life was beginning to seem mundane. She woke up, got the kids ready for school then kissed her husband goodbye and stared at the television all day. She was beginning to feel antisocial. She didn't take phone calls, didn't answer the door, she didn't even bother getting out of her room. She tried every trick in the book to get the thought of James out of her mind. She sat wallowing in self pity with a bucket full of ice-cream on her lap. She cried herself to sleep in the afternoon. She even went as far as drinking until she passed out.

Her husband noticed what was happening to her. He assumed it was just a passing phase; but when it lasted a whole fortnight he figured that something was out of the ordinary.

He came home from work late, Friday evening. He dropped his bag onto floor and walked up to his bedroom where he found Mia lying on the bed with a bottle of alcohol on her bedside that was nearly empty. He walked closer to see what had happened to her. He noticed that she had froth covering her lips and her fingers were trembling.

Bob sprang to the phone and dialed 911. He was in shock.

———— •◆• ————

The ride to the hospital was a bumpy and emotional one. Bob was seated by an unconscious Mia and two paramedics in an ambulance that was speeding with its siren on.

"Is she going to be okay?" asked a concerned Bob.

There was no response. Bob was getting frustrated; he was staring at the love of his life lay motionless on a stretcher with an oxygen mask on her face.

"Answer me, god damn it!" Bob yelled.

"Sir we're doing the best we can, will you please just remain calm." replied one of the paramedics.

Bob held Mia's hand and cried out loud, "Please baby, be alright. Please!"

The ambulance had come to a screeching halt. The nurses took Mia out of the ambulance and into the hospital. Bob ran behind them, he was concerned for her life. He was inflicting himself with self hatred. He believed that the reason she had done this to herself was the fights they'd been having. If only he had known what the real reason of her plight was.

Doctor William Smith walked up to Bob and greeted him.

"How is she, doc?" asked Bob.

"She's alright now; and should be up in a couple of hours." Replied William

"What happened to her?" Bob asked.

"Has your wife been having a drinking problem of late, Mister Camello?" asked the doctor.

Bob took a seat on one of the chairs in the waiting room. He had tears in his eyes as he said, "She never drank before our last fight." He paused as though he was waiting for a sign as to why she had become the way she had. He then went on to say, "She's become a zombie. All she does is stay home and drink by herself all day and night."

"Did you try stopping her?" asked Doctor Smith.

"I did for a while. Eventually I gave up." Said Bob, vexed.

"Mia has been diagnosed with severe alcohol poisoning. She'll be alright. Just keep her off the alcohol for a while." said William, as he patted Bob on the shoulder and went on to say, "Normally alcohol doesn't hit people as hard as this but she's been consuming a kind of alcohol far stronger than her body can handle."

"What do you mean, Doc?" asked Bob, puzzled.

William took a deep breath and asked, "Have you heard of 'The Green Fairy?'

———— • ◆ • ————

James sat on his couch and poured a drink into a shot glass. The shot glass was nearly full to the brim with a green alcoholic substance.

"You know what they say, Absinthe makes the heart grow fonder." said James, as he toasted; to himself.

'The Green Fairy' that Doctor William was referring to was Absinthe. A very potent alcohol with hallucinogenic properties, James had introduced this drink to Mia, early in their relationship.

He was trying to recall the first time that he had it with her. They were at a party at an abandoned warehouse. There was all sorts of illegal substances, from banned alcohol to every kind of drug there was, scattered all over the harem like environment. Mia had never been to a party of that sort before. She had always been curious as to what they were like; and she was amazed by what she saw. The warehouse looked like it had been abandoned. There was no furniture apart from two coffee tables in the centre of the room. One of them had all kinds of alcohol on it and the other had every imaginable kind of illegal narcotics. All over the place there were couples having sex, out in the open as though it was the normal thing to do. There were two large speakers at the opposite end of the shutter that acted as the entry gate. The room was dimly lit with red lights everywhere. Mia was sent into a trance the second she walked in and heard the loud music playing.

"Do you like the music?" James asked.

"Yeah, what is it?" asked Mia.

"Drum and bass, what you're listening to is the best of its kind." said James, bragging.

"Its great." said Mia, with a wide smile.

"It sounds better when you're high." said James as he escorted Mia to the alcohol.

James poured two shots of Absinthe into shot glasses. He gulped his glass down and stared at Mia. She didn't know what the drink was but she knew that whatever she did when she was with James made her feel more like what she always dreamed she would be; care-free.

The two of them had several shots and then proceeded to the table filled with drugs.

"Everyone here really does believe in 'sex, drugs and rock and roll.'" said Mia, as she stared at the many couples scattered around the place having sex.

"That's what these parties are all about. People with inhibitions come here to get rid of them, I don't see a better way to do that than to get wasted and fuck someone senseless." James replied.

Mia was impressed with James' take on life. She felt as though everything he said was true. It was as though he was a magician and everything he did or said had her more and more spellbound.

The two of them stood in the one of the corners of the room staring into each others eyes as they danced with their bodies pressed close to one another. Mia turned her back to James as she bucked her hips against James' pelvis. She caught the back of his hair and said, "I want you to free me of my inhibitions."

James pushed Mia forward and bent her down; she in turn arched her back. He lifted her skirt up to her lower back and dropped his pants. He held her hair back as he thrust in and out of her in sync with the music. James felt nothing but bliss and Mia felt cleansed of all her sins. It was the most satisfying sex they'd ever had.

The two of them awoke in each others arms at Mia's house the next morning. They had no recollection of how they had gotten there and of the events that had taken place the night before. Mia woke up because of the sunlight falling on her face. She looked around the familiar environment and was confused. She knew that she was at her house but what she didn't know was why James was in bed with her. "I must be dreaming." She thought to herself for a moment. But when reality kicked in she was in shock. She shook James in a desperate attempt to wake him up.

"James! You've got to get out of here!" she yelled.

Mia was panicking. Her husband was expected to be home soon and she wouldn't have anything to say to him if he saw James lying there beside her, naked.

"Where am I?" James asked in a very drowsy voice.

"You're in my fucking bed. I need you to get out of here!" Mia could feel her heart beat quicken. She felt as though it was going to pop out of her chest.

James stood up and wiped his face. He then went on to put on his clothes and kiss Mia on the forehead.

"I love you." He whispered.

"I love you too . . . Now get out of here!" she said as she spanked him, playfully.

"Ooh . . . in the mood for a recap already?" He said flirtatiously.

"For starters, we don't even remember if something did happen last night."

"Let me refresh your memory." He said as he leaned forward to kiss her.

She hurried through the kiss and broke free.

"What's the matter?" he asked, "Not good enough for you?"

"Different time and different place maybe?" she quipped.

He smiled and walked away, stopping by the door to blow her a kiss.

She smiled and swung her head back onto the pillow. She knew that the night that had transpired was magical. She could feel it, she just couldn't remember it.

———•◆•———

Mia awoke in the middle of the night. She looked around and found herself in an unfamiliar environment, surrounded by electronics. She knew she was in a hospital bed but she had no recollection of what had gotten her there. She felt paralyzed and she liked it. She didn't want to be bothered by anything at this point. After the weeks of drinking herself to sleep she had finally found what she wanted; peace and quiet.

The thoughts of self-hatred and the never-ending bickering by the voices in her head had come to a halt.

She looked around the room and found her husband asleep on the bed next to hers. She peeked outside the window and noticed it was dark outside; darker than she had ever seen the sky before. "It's always darkest before dawn." She thought to herself. To confirm her doubts she peered at the wall-clock in front of her; it read 3:30 AM. She had a long night to kill and sleep wasn't on her agenda.

She sat with her back upright, twiddling her thumbs for what felt like hours. She gazed at the clock, this time it read 3:43 AM. "Whatever happened to time flying when you're having fun?" she wondered.

Mia ran out of thoughts, with nothing to pacify her she turned to her memories. She thought of a few things that didn't involve James and then she had no choice but to think of all the fun times she had with him. She missed him dearly and even considered calling him. Sadly, there was more than just him that she missed. She missed the drugs even more. She wanted to feel like her feet were off the ground, she wanted to be reminded what it feels like to not have a care in the world. She needed James for that. James, and his drugs.

She realized it was a Saturday night, the night she usually spent with James. She was convinced now; the only way that she could enjoy a Saturday was when it involved James and getting high. She decided to honor their traditions even without drugs. She rocked her head back and forth to the tune of the music playing in her head. When she was fed up of playing 'make-believe' she gave up and rested her head on the pillow. All she thought of was drugs, sex and alcohol. "An idle mind is the devils workshop." She thought to herself. As it turned out, her mind was nothing if not idle.

———•◆•———

James was feeling more restless than he'd felt ever before. He stayed up all night thinking about the good times he shared with Mia. He couldn't stop thinking of her. He had left several messages on her cell phone but there was no response to any of them. Out of sheer depression, he sat on his bed staring out the window as he smoked marijuana. Suddenly he felt as though getting high didn't take away his pain. He needed something that would numb his mind completely. He stood up and walked towards the bathroom. He reached for whatever pills he could find and emptied out the bottle into his palm, as he filled up a glass of water. He stared at himself in the mirror and saw nothing. He thought philosophically and thought that the mirror is showing him the emptiness inside himself.

He put all the pills into his mouth at once and kept staring into the mirror. He then took a big sip of the water and gulped all the pills down at once. It felt as though the pills were fighting their way down his esophagus. He kept staring at the mirror and finally he saw himself in it. He figured that his life wasn't worth living without her. If she wasn't around, he had nothing to look forward to.

He let out a peaceful smile as he stared at himself, with a whole new perspective. That smile was followed by a loud thud, when James' head hit the cold and unforgiving bathroom floor.

CHAPTER 3

THAT'S THE WAY IT IS

The warm summer breeze caused Mia's hair to flow with the wind. Her feet were leaving impressions on the sand as she walked towards James. He stared at her as the waves gushed to the shore behind her. She walked closer to him and said, "Hello handsome." He in turn said, "You look beautiful today." She blushed and went on to say, "I want to live with you, I want to have babies with you!" James in shock said, "Pinch me. I'm dreaming." She smiled and said, "Okay." as she pinched his arm playfully. And that's when James woke up.

———— • ◆ • ————

James was in an unfamiliar place, he was on a single bed in a room that had no furniture other than an empty steel chair by the side of his bed. He looked at his arm; it had a needle in it. He looked under his blanket and found himself in a hospital robe. He knew the pills had gotten him there. He had hoped they would take him one step further and into his grave.

He pulled the needle out of his hand and walked out of the room. He saw a few doors opened with patients fast asleep. He treaded the corridors as though he knew where he was going, but in reality he hadn't a clue.

He passed several doors and saw different people sleeping; he noticed the pain on their faces. Every room he passed he noticed the patients in discomfort even as they slept. All except for one room; he stopped at the door and stared inside the room. The patient was a woman and she was smiling in her sleep. She looked beautiful. Not the typical definition of beauty but a charm that was so overwhelming, she'd leave a man speechless even when she was in a hospital gown. There was something different about the way she looked. She was perfect in James' opinion, just like Mia. He squinted and tried to see clearer, her hair was just like Mia's and her lips were just like hers too. It was only when he walked closer to her that he found it WAS Mia. James whispered her name, just to make sure. She didn't wake up. He took a step towards the room as he pushed the door open slowly. He felt his heart was beating fast. After all the days of trying to get a hold of her, after dialing her number frantically, he found her at the last place he'd expect to. He walked inside the room and felt someone holding him back. He turned around and found a blonde woman with a petite figure and big blue eyes. She was wearing a nurse's uniform. She looked at him and said, "What are you doing out of bed honey?" James was confused, "Do I know you?" he asked. She led him down the corridor towards his room and said, "I'm Amy. I've been nursing you back to health." James was drawn to her. He thought there was something charming about her. She brought him into his room and helped him get onto the bed. She smiled at him as she put the needle back into his arm. "We're here to help you. And I need you to know we can't do that if you're frolicking around like that."

"Won't happen again." James said reassuringly.

"Good. We wouldn't want the other nurses to see you walking down that corridor, bare-assed, now would we?" she flirted.

"No my love, that's a privilege reserved for you." he said, also flirting.

Amy blushed as she walked out of the room; James waited for the coast to get clear. He couldn't get out of bed in his bare-assed state when Amy was around. He feared that she'd escort him back to his bed and stick an ivy-drip in his veins. He sat up and pulled the needle out of his skin. This was something he had to do, to find himself and to find Mia.

He walked out to the door of his room and peered from the corner of his eyes on either corner of the long and dimly lit corridor. "The coast is clear." he whispered to himself as he tiptoed down the hallway towards the room where he had seen Mia. He walked into her room and gazed around, taking in whatever was happening around him. It was a feeling he'd never felt before. All of a sudden James was taken aback by life's funny ways. Karma had led the pills down his throat and into his stomach and those pills were the cause of him landing up in what he thought was the worst possible predicament he could land himself into. Fate would not have it for him to be destined for a lonely grave. He wound up in the same hospital where Mia was, just a few feet away from her. The same Mia he was longing for. The same Mia that refused to take his calls.

He walked into the room that she was in. He stood there staring down at her from atop her bedside. He played with her hair and left her a soft kiss on the cheek. She opened her eyes, slowly; as she stared into his. "Mia, whatever happened . . ." James tried to explain but Mia raised her finger up to his lips and in turn whispered, "You don't owe me an explanation. Whatever happened shouldn't have happened." Before he knew it, the two of them were sharing a passionate embrace. James went on to say, "Oh, but it did happen."

To which she said, "I sat here for the last few hours thinking of every happy thought I've had . . ." She stopped to wipe away the tears dripping down her cheeks, James began shushing her; "You'll wake up your husband!" James stared down at Mia's husband Bob as he lay face first on a bed next to Mia's. Mia ignored everything that came out of James' lips and went on to say, "I have no happy moments in my life that don't involve you."

James smiled at Mia. He knew the love of his life wasn't going to give up on him because of a mistake that he had made. "I love you, Mia. I have and always will give you all my love, sometimes more than I have to give." He said, with a hunger for love and lust in his voice. "I'll be out of here soon, then we can be together just like we used to." Mia added.

"Just like we used to." Said James with a wide smile on his face and a teardrop on his cheek.

"Are you going to sit there and talk all night or are you going to kiss me?" quipped an overwhelmed Mia.

James got to his knees and kissed Mia. This was the most passionate kiss either of them had ever been a part of. The kiss was broken a few seconds later. Mia went on to say, "Pinch me. I'm dreaming."

James pinched her and said, "Then I hope that it never ends."

———— •◆• ————

The next morning came by like a flash. Bob was rudely awoken by the rays of the sun peeking through the blinds; he wiped his face as he sat up and walked towards Mia's empty bed. He picked up a note that lay in the center of the bed on top of which rested Mia's wedding ring. Bob picked up the note in disbelief and read it. The note read:

Dearest Bob,

I wish there was another way to tell you this, but I'm afraid there isn't. You're probably wondering what brought on the sudden change in me. I promise you, every question that I had left unanswered will be answered for you by the end of this letter.

It's safe to say that we had problems from the very beginning. Sure the first few years flew by like a gust of wind, but it was the years after that which really began to become strenuous. You asked me for the longest time, "Why didn't you change your last name after we got married?" to which I replied with one thing, "I will when I feel the need to." The day has come where I must tell you this . . . you haven't given me a reason to want to. I thought I could be a mother to your children from your last marriage, turns out I was wrong. A woman feels complete when she becomes a mother; the fact of the matter is, Bob . . . You couldn't make me one. Call me ruthless, but your shooting blanks and prematurely at that, I can't even begin to tell you how hard it makes things for a being as sexual as myself. With this note I would like to tell you that I have wronged you and I can't do it anymore. My conscience won't let me. But really, what life are we living if we're forced to go through with it without being truly happy?

There's someone else. There has been for a long time. I don't want you to take this in the wrong way, but if you look at it closely what other way is there to take this? You're a great man and a wonderful father, and I'm sure that someday you'll make a woman feel like your sun sets and rises with her. We had a great run; but we didn't have the stamina to last. I'm saying everything so bluntly because I honestly don't want to hurt you anymore and I can't have you chasing after a ghost. I'm going to vanish from your life and I want you to let me. Pretend that I died; it's easy for me to say because I'm already dead on the inside. It goes without saying that I left in a hurry. I've found someone that can make me truly happy. I want to give things a shot with him. I won't be coming home tonight, or any night for that matter. Take care of yourself, Bob.

Love and regrets,

Mia.

PS: Now you can give this wedding ring to whoever deserves it. I know it was your mothers and it meant a lot to you; I'm sorry I couldn't be the one that carried forward her legacy.

Bob put the letter down and stared at the ring on the bed. He reached into his pocket and pulled out his cell-phone as he began dialing a number. He held the phone to his ear until he heard the ringing stop.

Once the phone had been answered he said, "Hey honey . . . I guess it's time we took things to the next level, no more faking poker nights on a yacht. I've left my wife to be with you."

CHAPTER 4

A Tale of Two Cities

"You know what they say, absence makes the heart grow fonder."
He said.

"Oh then I'm very, very fond of you." She said and the two of them
began to make sweet love to each other.

———•◆•———

A week had passed by since Mia had moved in with James. They
were both on the road to recovery and they were nursing each
other back to full health, one joint at a time.

When Mia came back into James' life he started painting again, his
living room was filled with different paintings. They were better
than he had ever painted before.

"Looks like you got your muse back." Mia quipped, when she
noticed James painting all day. James in turn returned a polite
smile and kissed her softly.

The two of them would spend all day painting together and at
night they'd go out on dates. Everyday was something new and

something more exciting than the last night. But every night had the same ending. Drugs.

Tonight was yet another date night for the two of them.

"What should we do today?" asked James.

"How about, we stay in tonight. Just you and me, like the old days." said Mia.

"Oh, that might be a problem." replied James.

"And why might that be?" asked Mia, vexed as ever.

"I've invited a friend over, I'm sure you'll like her." he said with a wicked grin on his face.

"If you think I'm having a threesome with you and a random girl, you're dead wrong. Well, for now at least." said Mia, playfully.

"I think this is the kind of threesome you'd enjoy" Said James as he pulled out a bag full of pills.

"There's always room for a little E." said Mia as she reached for the bag.

James pulled it away from her, "Not yet." He said, "That's dessert. Here's the appetizer." He said as he reached for another packet that had hashish in it.

"You're pulling all the stops tonight, honey!" she said, giggling like a child.

"You think so? Wait until you get to the main course." He said, chuckling.

———— • ◆ • ————

The two of them sat on the couch eating take out and smoking joints.

"Light another one." said Mia, "This one's got no gas in the tank."

"I'll make a deal with you. For every joint we smoke, you're going to have to tell me one thing about your past that you haven't told me before." James said, while stubbing out the remainder of the joint.

"I have a lot of skeletons in my closet, are you sure you can handle that?" said Mia, seriously.

"When I stole you away from your family I wanted you, I still want you. Skeletons and all."

Mia kissed him on his cheek and took the joint out of his fingers. She took a drag of it and smiled. "Are you sure you want to know about my life?" she paused and then went on to say, "I mean . . . I'd love to share it, but it could get a little intense."

"You should've thought about that before you took a hit." He said with a wry smile.

"Hey, no fair!" she quipped, "The deal was after every joint, not after every hit!"

"The rules have changed, my dear. Do you still want to play? I'd be happy to take the remainder of that joint away from you and have it all to myself." He said.

"Okay, but next time I make the rules." She replied while taking another drag.

"This story better be good." He said.

"Okay, here goes. This is back when I was a teenager; I was dating this boy, he was the kind of guy your parents would warn you not to be with." She said as she was interrupted by James.

"Really? I don't think I was even born then." He said.

"Oh shut up and listen, will you?" she said as she hit his chest softly, "So this boy, he was nineteen and I was only fourteen at the time. All the girls in the neighborhood were crazy about him. He had only just moved in. He noticed me and he made a pass at me and I was too much in awe of what was going on to understand any of what was going on. He took me out to dinner and a movie; I still remember it, 'The Bride of Dracula' it was called."

"Wasn't it 'The Bride of Frankenstein'?" James interrupted.

"Not the one I went to see. This movie only ran in drive-ins. We were having a great time and halfway through the movie he said something really sweet, I don't remember exactly what it was but I think he was saying something about my eyes." She said while reminiscing.

"So you fucked him?" James asked, curtly.

"I was young and he was the talk of the town. When a guy that good looking makes a pass at a younger girl and asks her to do it with him in the backseat of his fathers car, the girl can't say no!" she replied, bashfully.

"So your first time was with a guy you just met, in a drive-in movie theater?" James said while bursting into laughter.

"Don't be an asshole James, it was puppy love!" she said.

"More like puppy-lust. Did you do it in doggy style?" he asked, joking.

"As ironic as it sounds, yes." She said, as her cheeks turned pink.

"Poetic justice." He said.

"You're a real jerk, you know that?" she said wryly.

"I'm a jerk that you love, so I guess that makes me 'the' jerk." He replied as he leaned in to kiss her.

After the kiss was broken she took another hit of the hashish and had forgotten about the little game that they were playing.

"Aha! You owe me one more story now." James said.

"You're still not horrified by my teenage sexual escapades?" she said shyly.

"Sexual escapades? You fucked a guy in the backseat of a car, what's so great a story about that. Give me something really juicy." He said, mischievously.

"I don't have anything juicier to talk about than sex, and I didn't have a lot of it before I got married." She said while smoking the joint.

"Okay then, tell me about your life minus the sex. I want to know everything there is to know about you." He said while looking deep into her eyes.

"Are you sure you can't see right through me already?" she said while breaking eye contact.

"Oh, come on! I'm sure there are things you haven't told me yet." He said.

"Yeah, now that you mention it." She said, with seriousness in her voice.

"Spill it!" he said, eagerly.

"When I was sixteen my mother passed away and for a couple of years I couldn't deal with it. My father tried to get me out of depression. All his desperate attempts were to no avail. I didn't take it to well." She paused as she wiped the tears rolling down her cheek. She then went on to say, "I became anti-social and changed everything there was to change in my life. I redecorated the house, I took my work seriously; I did everything I could to divert my mind. The tragic part is that I didn't talk to a soul about what I was going through. My father knew what was going on and he'd do everything that he could in his power to snap me out of it, but nothing worked. Until one day when he came home with tickets in his hand and told me to pack my bags because we were going on a trip. I was skeptical at first but then I thought I owe him that much, at the very least. So I packed my bags and hopped into the car with him."

Mia was sent back in time, as she visualized every detail of what she was saying.

"Where are we going, dad?" Mia asked confused.

"Remember when you were twelve years old and your mother told you about the snow filled lands that she grew up in?" her father replied.

"Yes, it was somewhere in France, if I remember correctly." She said.

"Yeah, that's right. It's a place called Rouen." He said.

"Why would they name it Rouen if it's such a lovely place? Paints a bomb-shattered towns picture in my head." She said, with the least bit of enthusiasm possible.

"You'll change your mind when you get there, honey." Her father replied as he held her hand.

————◆————

"Did you change your mind?" asked James.

"I'm getting to that, hold your horses." Mia replied.

————◆————

She remembered the flight clearly, every second of it. All she did was stare out the window, looking down and the sea and different pastures of land as she traveled from one continent to the next. All she thought of how much her mother would have loved the trip they were taking. She found some happiness in knowing that her mother would be happy to know her daughter was going to her hometown. "This is for you mom." Mia thought to herself as she cried, quietly.

She was staring down at the runway that the aircraft was circling and thinking about how downtrodden this place was going to be. What she had envisioned was a grief-stricken place. She presumed that knowing about this place would make her miss her mother even more. Mia hadn't even gotten off the plane and she was already filled with a feeling of regret.

The flight came to an end as the plane came to a standstill. Her father stared at the seatbelt sign as he waited for it to go off. "I was here to study and I met your mother." He said with longing in his voice, "It was love at first sight. I thought that there was no one that could come close to as beautiful as she was." He said with tears in his eyes.

Mia looked at him in silence with a frown on her face, she missed her mother dearly.

"I was wrong about that." He said while wiping a tear off his cheek.

Mia was crying too, she had never seen her father cry. "Who did you find that was prettier than she was?" Mia asked, part enraged and part curious.

"My daughter." He said as he held his daughter in his arms and wept.

Mia couldn't help but cry with him. She knew her father was doing the best he could, she was feeling pathetic that she hadn't thought about what he was going through amidst all her inner fears. "I love you." He said, "Nothing is going to keep me away from you."

———•◆•———

James sat on the couch staring into Mia's tear glistened eyes. He hugged her tightly, as though he was never going to let go.

"You don't have to say anymore if you don't want to." James said to her.

"I've never really spoken about this to anyone, it feels great. I'd like to continue if that's okay with you?" she asked, politely.

James couldn't help but nod; he had never seen Mia so emotional about anything.

———•◆•———

The second Mia got off the flight and her feet touched the ground she was taken aback. She felt as though her feet were off the ground. It was the most positive she'd ever felt in over a year.

The sights that she was looking at were everything but what she had imagined. She hadn't even gotten off the runway and she knew that this place was special. The air was crisp and the weather was cool. The sun was peeking through clouds, teasing the birds and bees with warmth. Mia was smiling again. Her father looked at her and smiled with her. The two of them were happy. Neither of them thought that this would ever be a possibility.

The time they spent in Rouen was nothing if not sheer bliss. Mia's father took her to every place that he had ever gone to with his wife. Mia would sit with him at the same tables at the same restaurants that her mother once went to. She felt a warmth fill up inside her every time her father took her to some place new and told her the story behind its significance. She knew that her mother once sat exactly where she was sitting at that moment. She knew that her mother was happy at that very moment.

"I think it's about time I told you this Mia." Said her father with a smile on his face.

"Yes, daddy?" replied Mia.

"Your mother told me, before she passed away that she always wanted to see you happy. Since the day that you were born, you didn't disappoint her. Not once. She wanted you to grow up to be the kind of girl that could do things her own way and at her own pace. She told me that I'd know when the time was right and when it was that time to bring you here and take you to all the places I've taken you."

"She knew." said Mia, with a wide smile.

"She knew what?" asked her father, baffled.

"She knew it would be the only thing that would make me feel connected to her." She paused and went on to say, "I love you dad!" as she jumped into his arms and hugged him.

"I love you too sweetheart. This place isn't just mine and your mothers. It's yours too now. Every time you're feeling gloomy about any situation, come here and it'll clear the blues in a jiffy." He said, while giving her warm parental advice.

———— • ◆ • ————

"Did you ever go back there?" James asked.

"No, I didn't have to. I found you" Mia replied with a smile.

"Yeah, I'm here to ruin your life anyway." James said, cheekily.

Mia giggled and said, "You always know what to say to make me laugh."

"I also know how to get you to have a very intense orgasm." James said, flirtatiously.

"I beg to differ." Mia said, with a wry smile on her face.

"Oh, do you now?" James responded while he leaned in to kiss her.

CHAPTER 5

CRUSH AFTER USE

"She left without saying a word to me." He said, the pain in his voice was imminent.

"Not a word?" She asked, while caressing his bare chest.

"She left me a letter." He quipped.

"You must be devastated. You poor baby! What can I do to help you?" She asked, flirtatiously.

"A pity fuck would be nice." He said.

"I would honey, but it's a pity that you can't fuck." She replied.

"Premature ejaculation is a serious problem and I don't appreciate you making jokes about it! Stupid bitch!" Bob yelled.

"Premature what? You've got to get to work!" yelled the blonde girl by his bedside whose name he barely remembered. "I'm leaving. Don't ever call me again."

"Oh why do you have to be this way, Sarah? It wasn't my fault." He retorted as he lay flat on his back as she got up off the bed and began getting dressed.

She was walking towards the door and heading out without saying anything.

"Way to go Sarah, walk out on me without saying anything, you're just like my wife. All women are the fucking same!" he yelled.

"My name is Jamie, you asshole!" she yelled as she stormed out the door.

"Jamie?" he said confused, "Where the fuck is Sarah?" he asked out loud.

"Are you high?" Jamie asked absolutely dumbfounded. Soon after saying those words she left Bobs apartment.

Bob wrapped the blanket around his waist and began walking towards the bar in the living room. He set aside a stout, thick glass and filled it up to the brim with ice, then poured fine scotch all over the ice; some of the ice melted. Bob liked looking at the ice melt. To him it felt as though the ice was a metaphor for what he really is, Tough on the outside, but really weak and fragile when being handled. The scotch to his mind was Mia, the one thing he could never get enough of, the one thing that would eventually be the death of him.

———— • ◆ • ————

Bob had fallen asleep on the couch. He spent the day drinking until he passed out. He would have stayed asleep all day if it hadn't been for the doorbell being rung persistently.

He walked towards the door slowly, as though he had no bones in his body. Everything around him was hazy and the ground beneath him was spiraling out of control. He answered the door.

"Mia!" he exclaimed, "You came back for me. I knew you'd come back!" he said as he reached to hug her.

Mia didn't return the hug. Bob was weeping on her shoulder, everything he said was impossible to decipher.

Mia pushed him off gently and said, "I'm not here to get back with you, I'm here to pick some of my stuff up."

"Why are you so heartless? Was I so cruel to you that I deserve this punishment?" said a heartbroken and distraught Bob.

Mia was oblivious to the feelings Bob was experiencing; she felt no remorse or pity. All she could think of was how badly she wanted to get out of there and get back to James. "Have you been drinking?" Mia asked in a futile attempt to make small talk.

"No! I think it's preposterous that you even make that assumption!" Bob slurred.

"No it isn't. The stench of it on your breath is what's preposterous."

"Okay, I've been drinking. You're one to talk about it you fucking hypocrite!" Bob yelled, disrespectfully.

"I don't want to get into this with you, I'm just going to take my shit and leave." Mia replied as she walked passed him and towards the bedroom.

"I hope you fucking burn in hell. I hate you!" Bob yelled, as he burst into tears.

"I'm glad you feel that way." Mia said as she walked even further away.

"Mia stop . . . wait!" Bob yelled, desperately.

"What is it, Bob?" Mia asked, frustrated.

"I love you!" he said as he fell to the floor crying like a child that had been denied attention.

Mia walked away as she whispered, "And he says I'm the fucking hypocrite."

James sat in his apartment wondering where his paintings had disappeared. He had scanned through the entire apartment thoroughly and he hadn't a clue where they were.

"Mia must've sold them without telling me!" he thought to himself.

He tossed pillows around the living room hoping that Mia had put them away without his knowledge, alas; he was left without a trace of them.

James was getting frustrated of looking, he needed some money and he needed it quick. He thought that selling a few of his old paintings would give him enough to buy some more drugs. It was only twelve hours ago that he had bought something new, something experimental, for Mia and himself. The two of them had never done it before and he thought that it would be an exciting day with a twist if they were to be on it. James had already taken a little bit of it to test it out.

For James this feeling was new, unlike any other he had felt in recent times. He was staring at a light bulb but couldn't see light coming out of it; instead he saw the 7 colours of the rainbow flying out at him as though the elements that the light was composed of broke down into individual parts. It was one of the most beautiful things he had ever seen, if not the most beautiful. When he looked away from the light the room and all his surroundings began to develop a faint purple hue. Everything had engulfed itself in the tint. James sat back on the couch that he had thrown apart in an attempt to find his paintings.

———·◆·———

Mia walked into the room a few hours later only to find James flat on his back with his eyes shut. The house was a complete mess, there were feathers all over the place and torn pillows and embroidery scattered on the ground. Even the coffee table in the middle of the living room was in pieces on the floor.

Mia walked up to James and slapped his cheeks lightly.

"James, wake up!" she said as she stirred his motionless body.

"Huh? What?" James said as he came to

"What the fuck happened, are you alright?" she asked, concerned.

James sat up and wiped his eyes. He looked around the room and was taken aback.

"What the fuck?" he said out loud.

"My sentiments exactly." Mia responded.

"My paintings? Where are they?" James exclaimed.

"You put them in your closet! Is that what this is all about?" Mia was getting very concerned with James' behavior.

James sat there without saying a word. Mia looked at him with disgust.

"You took that LSD didn't you?" she looked at him waiting for an answer

"That guy told me its supposed to make you mellow; I didn't know . . ." He was cut short

"What guy, James? Who are these fucking people! I told you not to do that or any other shit when you're alone because . . ." She too was cut short.

"Because what Mia? Because I'm a fucking wreck and you don't trust me to be left alone?" James burst into tears

"James, don't do this." Mia said while rubbing off the headache that was building its way up.

"It's done. I'm sorry. You were right and I was wrong." James stood up and walked towards the door.

"Where the fuck do you think you're going James!" Mia yelled as she stood up.

"I need some space, I don't know who you are anymore, I don't know who I am anymore and quite frankly I don't know what anything is anymore." He responded as he opened the door.

"Baby! That's not true, you know me and I know exactly who you are!" Mia said.

"Oh yeah? And what is that exactly?" He asked while wiping the tears rolling down his cheeks.

"You're my life support." Mia sat back down the second the words escaped her lips. She wasn't the sort that would let her emotions get the better of her, not usually anyway. This time things were different. Tears rolled down her eyes as though someone had carved a gaping hole through the heart of a reservoir.

James walked back into the living room and closed the door behind him. He took a seat next to Mia and held her quivering body in his arms.

"Don't say that." James said.

"Say what?" Mia said without looking up

"That I'm your life support. That would mean that you're fucked up." James smiled.

"No, you're fucked up." Mia said as she let out a faint smile.

"Agreed, but not as fucked up as you are." James said as Mia lifted her head off his chest and looked into his eyes.

"I love you." She said.

"Why, thank you." He replied.

Mia hit him softly on the shoulder, "Asshole." She went on to say.

They looked into each others eyes for a few seconds and kissed each other soon after. When the kiss was broken Mia said, "If you could just lay off the drugs for a little while we could both live happily ever after."

"Happily ever after it is then." James said.

CHAPTER 6

HAPPILY EVER AFTER

"They call it stormy Monday." Mia said as she put on her pants to get ready for a job interview.

"But Tuesday's just as bad." James said as he stubbed the cigarette that he was smoking while he was still in bed.

———————◆————

Mia and James had lots of free time on their hands, now that drugs weren't a medium to kill time for the two of them. They appeared to be happier than before now that the two of them had gotten rid of their vices. They were doing things that normal couples would do; they went out on dinner and movie dates and sometimes they even spent romantic evenings at home. Even though the two of them loved spending time with one another they didn't know what to do anymore. Two weeks had passed since their last hit and by now they'd had enough of each other. Mia suggested taking up a job and James liked the idea. They could use a little financial aid and a job would be more consistent than waiting on James to be inspired. Paintings weren't going to paint themselves.

Mia had an attractive resume before she had been married; she always had an eye for journalism. In her teens she had always wanted to be remembered for starting revolutions and shedding light on false policies. But when she became a wife and stepmother she had forgotten all those ideals and principals. Everything else in her life played second fiddle. She remembered when she was in school and how she was the editor of the school newspaper. Her words had a resounding impact on her intellectual peers. She tossed all that away only to wake up at six in the morning and get breakfast ready for children that weren't even hers and for a husband she didn't even love. She chose James over all that because he never pressured her into doing something she didn't want to. She could be herself around him and she could do whatever she pleased. She had lined up an interview at a local newspaper and decided to start off as an intern. If she had gotten this job she wouldn't have an extraordinary pay-slip but she'd be doing what she always wanted to do.

"Right . . . Mrs. Camello?" Said the balding man sitting in front of Mia as he tossed a file on the table.

"Miss. Yes. How are you today?" She responded.

"Well, thank you. It says here you are in your mid-thirties?" he said, sternly.

"Why, yes?" She said confused.

"You're not married. Does that have anything to do with the fear of committing to something?" he said, his voice lacked humanity and concern.

"With all due respect, I thought this was a job interview." Mia responded.

"That it is. At this firm we like to know our possible employees on a more personal level." He was sounding more and more like a drone to Mia. She was amazed at how someone could say things that could hurt someone emotionally without even flinching. *That's part of his job* she thought to herself.

"If it's alright with you, I'd like to keep my personal life personal." She said just as curtly.

"As you please." He said as he began asking her questions that were more work related.

James had a lot of free time on his hands. In the past he wouldn't have known what to do with himself if he didn't have drugs to resort to. He was staring at a blank canvas for over half an hour and no inspiration had struck him. He was staring at the canvas as though it were a reflection of himself. He felt empty.

He had a wooden palette in his hand; around the edges were the primary colors. The center of the palette was empty so that he could blend those colors to make secondary ones. He stared at the palette for long before he had been struck with inspiration. He began sinking his brush into the colors and blending them together. He painted for what seemed like hours.

Mia had finished her interview and was on her way home. Her tentative new workplace was twenty minutes from where James and her resided. On her journey back home she had a lot of time to think about what the seemingly coldblooded interviewer had to say.

'You're in your mid-thirties and your not married? That's odd.' His cold tone was playing on and on in her mind as though the vinyl was moving but the stick had remained still in its place. She was thinking about why James and she had not taken it to the next level. They knew they loved each other. Mia doubted that the relationship she was in was the real deal. As she parked her car she decided that she would talk about this at length with her better half once she reached the apartment.

She walked up the spiraling staircase that lead to the place she called home and opened the door only to find James sitting a few feet away from a canvas with paint all over his clothes. He kept staring at it ignoring Mia's presence. Mia walked over to the canvas and was stupefied by what she was seeing. It was the most beautiful painting that she had ever seen in her life. The background consisted of a soulful blend of Blues, Yellows and Reds and the foreground consisted of many different shapes and abstract designs in dark and well-balanced colours.

"Oh my god, James! That's amazing!" she said with tears in her eyes as she pounced onto him and held him tight.

"Is it?" he responded.

"Of course it is!" She confirmed, "It's the most depth I've ever seen in any painting." She wasn't lying about that.

He smiled and said, "How did your meeting go? Did you get it?"

"It was alright, I guess." She shrugged, "They said they'd get back to me." Mia knew at the back of her mind that she wasn't going to get the job. What scared her was the fact that she was blaming her loose-ended relationship with James for it.

"That's good news. If you don't get it then it's their loss. You're a genius!" he said as he kissed her gently on her cheek.

Mia smiled and walked away from the room. She was beginning to forget everything that the interviewer had said. She remembered why she was so in love with James. "You should keep at it; you're getting really good!" she said as she walked into the bedroom.

James sat there staring at the canvas; to his eyes it was still blank.

———— •◆• ————

Mia had gotten out of the shower and walked back into the living room. She found James at the door talking to the same skimpily clad woman that she had seen him with a few months ago. She was enraged but she kept her composure as she began eavesdropping on the conversation.

"Baby, why do things have to be this way? Come on out and play . . . Do a little coke with me and I'll open my arms, mouth and pussy to show my gratification." Said Jennifer.

"I'm clean Jen. I already have arms to crawl into; I don't need you." He said to her. Mia, who had been listening intently from a position that was out of sight, was elated.

"I need you James! I want you!" She said as she reached closer to him and bit her lips.

"If you don't leave now I'll be forced to slam the door shut on you." James said as he turned his face away, trying to dodge a kiss that Jennifer had been trying to plant on him.

"Was this all a fucking lie? The sex? The drugs? You and me? Us?" She started yelling.

"Yes." James said, "It was all a figment of your imagination."

"Fuck you! I hope you burn in hell. You and that bitch that's taking you away from me!" She said, in tears.

James drew closer to her with his posture upright and said, "If you call her that one more time I will throttle your neck so hard that whatever little is left of that fucked up brain of yours will pop open at the seams." The rage in his voice was prominent.

"Go ahead and strangle me! If I don't have you I may as well die!" she said, weeping.

"Get out. You'll be hearing from my lawyers, I don't want to see you within a 100 mile radius of me." He said as he slammed the door shut.

James walked back into the living room and Mia pretended to walk in at the same time.

"Hey you." He said as he looked at Mia, all smiles.

Mia smiled back at him. "Hey yourself." she said cheekily, "I heard some noise, everything alright" she added.

"Yeah, everything's fine." He said as he sat on the couch and flipped on the television set. No sooner did he do that than moans and groans came flying out of the speakers. He scrambled for the remote control to flip the channel.

"Really? Porn?" Mia asked him as she smiled wryly.

"I d-don't know what that . . ." he was cut short.

"Leave it on." Mia said as she picked a spot next to James.

James looked at Mia, confused. He was happy; but confused nevertheless. 'I must be the luckiest man in the world!' he thought to himself.

———— •◆• ————

Bob had taken some time off from his business. He wanted to stay at home and be with his girlfriend; the same one that he had been meeting on weekend while Mia thought he was playing cards on a yacht. Time and again he'd think about what Mia would've thought if she had found out about his affair; little did he know that their marriage was more of an open relationship than he assumed. Sometimes he'd even think about telling her, hoping to double her sorrow.

Bob was happier now; he was even beginning to move on. He never wanted his affair to become a relationship but things changed for him far too quickly. His girlfriend was attractive, of course not as attractive as his ex-wife. She was smart, funny and had a charming personality; she still failed to fill the void that Mia had left. Bob was staring at an empty space on a wall filled with photographs that were dear to him, the empty space used to have a large photograph framed with brass of his kids, Mia and himself. That was another void that he was unable to fill.

"Hey honey." Said a blonde woman who crept up behind Bob and kissed his cheek.

"Hey Ashley, you scared me!" Bob responded while clutching his chest.

"I'm sorry. I just wanted to tell you that I'll have a bath running in a couple of minutes, would you care to join me?" she said, flirtatiously.

"Well, I was going to go and play golf..." He said cheekily

Ashley looked at him in disbelief and said, "Why would you want to swing your own club when I'm offering to swing it for you?"

"Okay okay, only if you promise to show me your birdie." He responded

"That depends on whether or not you'll show me your eagle." She said

"Are you sure you can handle my 9-iron?" he quipped.

"Are you going to make golfing puns all day or are you going to fuck me?" she said while cutting to the chase.

Bob started undoing his belt buckle as Ashley smiled and dragged him to the bathroom. 'I must be the luckiest man in the world!' he thought to himself.

CHAPTER 7

BLOW

"What are we supposed to do now?" James said.

"I've got nothing left to share with you." Mia said.

"Are we really happy without drugs?" James said softly.

Mia said nothing.

———•◆•———

James and Mia had been off drugs for a while and they had been fighting a lot more than they normally would. It started off fine but things went downhill after a while. There was only so much that they could talk about and for a few days they suddenly began ignoring each others presence in the room. If they had a choice they wouldn't have it be so, but it was a joint decision. They wanted to stay off drugs and do something with their lives. The question that posed itself upon them was how would they do something with their lives?

James couldn't paint anymore. His vision was tainted because his thoughts were clearer and he needed his mind to shut down so that he could paint that one string of thought on a canvas. Whereas Mia couldn't land herself a job for more reasons than one; as if that weren't enough she began noticing her beauty slipping away.

She spent hours staring at herself in the mirror, her voluptuous body was rapidly reducing to just skin and bone. James had too many thoughts on his mind to give attention to Mia, she thought he wanted nothing to do with her anymore because she wasn't as attractive as she used to be.

Mia decided it was time to spice things up, she wanted to prove to James and herself that she was still beautiful. She decided to go shopping for lingerie.

She tried on several outfits at the store and she saw something that scared her in her reflection. She was aging; losing weight and her beauty had vanished. She was disgusted with how she had become. She tried on almost everything in the store and nothing seemed to complement her body. After what seemed like hours of searching, she found a black negligee laced with tassels' of gold that she really liked.

She decided to trust her instincts and buy it.

"That'll be $150. Is there anything else I can help you with?" said the lady behind the cash register.

Mia opened her purse, stumbled through it rummaging for whatever currency she could find, and found nothing in it.

"Oh, I . . . I . . ." Mia tried to find words that would hide the shame that she was feeling but she couldn't.

The cashier just took the outfit and put it back on the rack and ignored Mia completely.

Mia swallowed her pride and walked out of the store with her head down. She got home to find James watching television in the same position he was in when she left the house.

"Hi?" Mia said.

James didn't respond.

Mia walked away into another room and yelled into a pillow just seconds before she burst into tears.

———— •◆• ————

After hours of doing nothing James went into the room to find Mia holding her head sitting there in the dark with mascara rolling down her cheeks.

"What the fuck is going on Mia?" James yelled

Mia looked up at James and cried loudly.

"You brought this on yourself! You wanted to stay sober! Look what it's done to us?" James was furious that Mia was portraying herself as the victim.

"I didn't know that you'd change so much!" Mia said, still in tears.

"How the fuck have I changed?" James said, confused.

"When was the last time you even looked at me? When was the last time we had sex, James!" Mia looked into James' eyes and she knew that he could feel her pain.

"Maybe if you tried hard enough . . ." James murmured as he was cut off

"How the fuck am I supposed to try? I don't have any money! We're fucking broke!" Mia walked out of the room and sat on the couch in the living room.

James followed her closely and then sat down next to her; "What are we supposed to do for money? I can't work without drugs." He said that calmly, knowing that he was out of line when he was yelling at her.

Mia picked up a cigarette from the table and lit it. She scratched her head as she thought about something for a while.

James twiddled his thumbs and said nothing. He had been over this in his head and he came up with nothing. "This blows." He said.

Mia blew the smoke out of her mouth and stared at James. "That's it!" she said as though she was struck by inspiration.

"Am I missing something?" James said.

"You're miserable without drugs, I'm miserable without drugs and we have no money!" Mia said, a smile was growing on her face.

"I think it's safe to say that that's already been established." James said, trying to cut the tension.

"No! Listen to me; we've got to start pushing." Mia was grinning from ear to ear.

"Pushing?" James thought Mia was talking in cryptic code, it was becoming harder and harder for him to understand what Mia was talking about.

"Dealing! We could sell the drugs. No one in this wretched city knows as much about drugs as you do! We'll find out what our competition is selling at and we can sell it for cheaper!" Mia held James' hands in hers and stared into his eyes with affection; she liked the fact that a smile was building on James' face when he began thinking about it.

"Let's do it!" he said, as he began kissing Mia on her neck and cheeks.

Mia moaned softly as James' lips moved up to hers. He kissed her passionately and ripped off her top. Mia in turn began unbuttoning his Jeans as he unhooked her bra.

Mia was sent into a frenzy, it had been so long since the two of them had shared any intimacy. The two of them rolled over off the couch onto the ground. James got on top of Mia and looked into her eyes, feasting off the pleasure that she was getting out of this act. The two of them were connected once again; Mia's entire body was being pushed to and fro on the ground because of James' motions.

When it was over, the two of them lay next to each other on the ground holding one and other as though they never wanted to let go.

———— •◆• ————

When Mia woke up there was no one in the apartment. She got up off the ground, thinking for a second, trying to remember why she had slept there; and when her memories came gushing back to her she smiled.

She decided to make herself some coffee; halfway through making it James walked in the door with a briefcase in his hand.

"Hey you." Mia blushed as she looked away. She felt like she was a teenager again, she slept with the same man that walked into the room and she couldn't look at him without blushing the morning after.

"Guess what I went and did." James smiled as he tossed the briefcase on the coffee table and began opening it.

"What is it?" Mia sprang to the couch before he unveiled it.

James opened the briefcase; it was filled with plastic packets filled with a white powdery substance.

Mia looked at it and instantly her face lit up. She jumped towards James and hugged him with all the strength she could muster.

"Where did you . . . ? How did you . . . ?" Mia was so ecstatic she couldn't finish a sentence.

"Never mind all that, do you want to sample the product?" James looked at her as he waved a tiny packet at her.

Mia sat there like a puppy dog that had just been teased with a bone.

"Open it!" she exclaimed.

James happily obliged, he spread the powder onto the table and began dividing it into thin lines.

Mia couldn't wait to get her hands on it. It had been so long without drugs that she had forgotten what it felt like. She lowered her head and brushed off the hair from her cheeks as she leaned in to snort it.

"Not so fast." James said.

Mia looked up at James with disgust; she thought he was teasing her.

James scanned through his pockets and pulled out a metal stem.

"The old coke straw! Nice touch." Mia said as she took it from him.

Mia set the straw at the bottom of one line and within seconds sniffed it through the straw.

She smiled and moved on to the next line.

"Save some for me!" James said, as he brushed her hair aside.

Mia snorted another line and looked up at James and said, "You might have to fight me for it."

James smirked and replied by saying, "Oh, if I have to resort to that, I will."

———— •◆• ————

Mia was walking in a meadow, she was smiling and looking behind her back and running away from someone playfully. She felt as though she was a child again, wearing a frilly white sundress. When she ran she could feel the warmth of the rays of the sun caressing her bare arms. James was chasing after her, he however; wasn't smiling. They ran around trees and shrubs, almost in circles chasing after each other. Mia ran far ahead of James' reach. She stopped and turned around to look for him but he was nowhere in sight. She turned back around and saw her ex-husband Bob Standing in front of her.

"I will never stop loving you." He said to her as he reached forward and kissed her.

Mia sat up in the bed, her palms and forehead drenched with sweat. She looked around and noticed she was in James' house.

"Thank god it was only a dream." She thought to herself. When she rested her head on the pillow again she began thinking about what Bob was doing. "What if he still loves me?" she thought.

———•◆•———

"Oh I stopped loving her the day she left me." Bob told his girlfriend, Ashley.

"Why are we talking about your ex-wife again, honey?" She asked puzzled.

"I mean, I don't think that she even knows what emotions are! How did I marry the bitch in the first place?" Bob ignored what Ashley said and went on talking about his feelings.

"She just left, she left a fucking note!" he said, whining.

Ashley got up off the bed and began getting dressed.

"Where are you going? It's the middle of the night!" Bob yelled

"I'm going to leave you here to figure your shit out. I'll see you tomorrow. Hopefully by then you'll be over the bitch that walked all over you." she responded as she walked out the door.

"I love you!" he yelled.

"At least she didn't say goodbye on a fucking post it." he said to himself.

CHAPTER 8

HOME IS WHERE THE ART IS

"This is fun and all James, but when do you plan on making money off this?" She asked.

"Why bother about money when you're so busy having fun?" He replied.

———— •◆•• ————

Mia and James had found their inner peace again. They felt as though they had done away with their demons by simply embracing those demons. The world was their oyster again, the drugs made it so. James was painting again, not on a canvas but on the walls of his room. Mia and him had found a fun way to get James back in the groove. They'd take paint and splatter it all around the walls of the place they called home.

The whole house was wrapped in plastic, the carpets, the furniture; everything was all neatly covered with plastic.

"The trick to being a good artist is, you've got to know what you're working with." James said.

"Wow, you're either more stoned than I am right now, or you have no idea what it is that you're talking about." Mia quipped.

"Shut up. I'm being serious." The second James said that, was the second Mia's smiley face turned into a sincerely interested one.

James was looking at the ripples of different shapes, sizes and colors all across the wall. Analyzing them, trying to get a new perspective.

Mia stared at James as he stared at the already painted wall.

"Hand me the bucket of yellow." He said. He sounded possessed; possessed by a passion. He had an epiphany.

He dipped his brush into the yellow paint bucket and splattered it all around the already kaleidoscopic living room.

The wall was now covered in swirls of purple, laced with blues of every hue and slides of blood red. In James' mind the yellow was all that was needed to tie it all together.

He stared at his work and smiled.

Mia stared at him and smiled.

"Want to go get fucked up now?" Mia asked.

"Okay!" James replied, all too quickly.

———•◆•———

The two of them lay in bed, their clothes covered in paint. Their pupils dilated and they had equal sized grins.

Mia was resting her head on his chest and he was toying with three specific strands of her hair, staring out of the tiny window in his bedroom.

"You make me happy." she said, as she rubbed her cheek against his nipple. The tingling sensation it caused came hand in hand with his nipples becoming erect.

"You make my nipples happy." he said. They burst into laughter shortly after.

"No, but seriously. Even though we're so horribly wrong for each other, deep down inside I know you're right for me." She said, still rubbing his chest.

"I love you and all, but it's hard to have a serious conversation with you when all you really want to do is play with my nipples." James said, playfully.

Mia sat up and sighed, "You think everything's a fucking joke! I'm pouring my heart out to you!"

James glanced away from the window and fixed his eyes on hers.

"Look at me . . ." he said, "Do these look like the eyes of someone that doesn't love the living daylights out of you?"

Mia knew he wasn't bullshitting. After all she knew James' tell. He'd never look someone in the eye if he was lying to them.

Mia smiled and ruffled his hair.

"Come back . . . We miss you." James said, looking at Mia while pointing towards his chest.

Mia tossed a pillow at him and said, "You're a fucking asshole."

James tickled her until she decided to rest her head on his chest again. He kissed her on the head, gently, as he thought about the rest of his life with her. The future looked good to him . . . Almost as good as the living room did.

Mia and James cuddled the evening away, they drifted off into a sound sleep as the sun went down and made way for night. They slept through most of it, unhindered but were rudely awoken by a vigorous knocking on the door.

James crawled out of bed with his blanket wrapped around his waist and got to the door, squinting at a scrawny black man in front of him.

"Hey man, I know it's early and all . . . but I heard you got some Charlie you're looking to sell?"

James looked at the clock on the kitchen wall. The minute hand was on 11 and the little hand was on 6.

"Look man. I need the fix! You going to hook me up or not?" The man in front of James wasn't playing around.

James scratched his hair confused, "Who told you about where to . . ." he was cut off

"I found you, that's all that matters. Do you have the coke or not?" the man was getting impatient.

"How much do you need?" James asked.

"How much you got?"

The second the man said that was the second James had to pinch himself to not let his excitement ooze out.

James shut the door halfway, leaving only a crack, which the man was trying to peep in through.

James picked up a cigarette from the table next to the briefcase and bought the briefcase filled with cocaine to the door.

"I've got enough. Now tell me how much you really need." James said, flaunting what he had in his hand.

The man leaned towards the side of the door and picked up a briefcase of his own. He held it in one hand and opened it with the other, revealing stacks of money.

"Like I said . . . I want all of it." He said.

James nodded in approval. Handed the man the briefcase in exchange for the briefcase that he carried.

"Pleasure doing . . ." James was cut off.

"Yeah, whatever." The man said as he walked away.

James shut the door and sat the briefcase down on the dining table. He opened it and stared at it for a long while, still in disbelief. He ran into the room to wake Mia up. He shook her until she opened her eyes, reluctantly, and looked at him.

"Mia! Slap me!" he said while kneeling over her.

"Wake me up one more time and I might." She said. As she ignored him and tried going back to sleep.

"I sold all the coke!" he exclaimed, like a little boy that just met the tooth fairy.

Mia's eyes were wide open now. "You w-what?" she said

"I sold it all!" He said, his smile now wider.

"Shut up!" she said as he nodded. She kissed him on his lips with more passion than ever before. The two of them were so excited. They believed that luck was finally favoring them.

Mia kept kissing him, as he lay on top of her, she pulled off the blanket that he was using to cover himself up and he yanked off her top.

"Fuck me." she said, staring into his eyes invitingly.

James smiled and said, "Hold on there's one thing I've got to do first." as he got out and ran back into the living room.

Mia was laying there confused for a few seconds, but James had returned with the briefcase filled with money and showered it on her and the bed.

"What are you doing?" Mia said as she giggled uncontrollably.

"I've always wanted to fuck a girl on a bed of money." He said.

And that he did.

Mia and James decided to take a walk together, to revisit some of their old 'happy places'. They walked along the road that led to a park, they sat on a bench staring at the sky and the birds flying by. They even spotted the sunset from their favorite rooftop. They did all the things that they would do together before they began living together. Well, minus the sex.

The hustle and bustle of the day had given way to the downpour of silence and nothingness that only the night can offer. The two of them, still hand in hand, walking along merrily as though all the world was a carnival. Just as they walked along the curb towards their house James spotted the same black man that bought cocaine from him earlier. James whispered in Mia's ear, "Come on, I want you to meet the guy that's going to change our lives." He took her hand and jogged with her towards the man in front of their apartment building.

"Hey! You! Briefcase dude!" James said, chuckling to himself.

"Hey," The man said, "It's you. Cocaine dude."

James looked around for suspicious ears, but he didn't find any. Regardless, he decided to hush the man up, "Shh! Not so loud, the whole world doesn't know us as dealers."

"Well, they're about to. Your coke was so good; I had to go around telling everyone about it. The way I see it, you were basically giving that stuff out for free. What a bargain!"

Mia and James were chuffed. She tugged on James' shoulder like a little child, giggling and smiling. They were proud of themselves. What better compliment for a dealer than to hear about his customers' satisfaction with the product?

"Anyway, I live nearby and I came by to ask if you guys had any more stuff on you." The man was rubbing his hands together to fight the cold air blowing down the street.

"More? Already?" James asked, almost giving out his excitement, but he managed to contain himself. "Yeah, I mean . . . I can arrange for some more. How much do you need?"

The man was walking away again, he said, "How much can you get?" and smiled, coyly.

James gave him a thumbs up with an approving nod

"Swing by to the chain link fence of the park you were walking by earlier today."

Mia stood there analyzing what the man had just said. How did he know they were at the park? Were they being followed? She looked over at James but he seemed unperturbed by all that had happened. He was busy trying to calculate something in his head.

Mia looked over at James who was now haplessly showing signs of elation. "Did you not hear him admit to stalking us, or did I imagine it?" She asked him, concerned.

"I heard no such thing." James said, counting on his fingertips.

"He said, 'the park you were at earlier.' You know that means he knew we were there!"

James looked deep into Mia's eyes, held her shoulders and said, "He said he lives nearby. He could've been around the area at the time. Even if he is following us; who cares?! He wants our coke and he's paying for it in cash-money! I'd sell parts of my body for cash-money!" he said, joking.

"I bet you have too." Mia said, playing along with his antics to show that she was on board with James' theory.

James walked over to a phone booth and told Mia to wait outside. She did. Contemplating escape routes as hostile thoughts fluttered through her mind. Why did the man know they were at the park? Even if James' theory was accurate, there's still a question of why this mysterious man, whose name hadn't even been mentioned in general conversation, didn't walk up and say hello. All that James knows of this man is that he pays good money for their cocaine.

James walked out of the phone booth before Mia could finish calculating the authenticity of this buyer.

"Right, so the coke's been arranged. What say we swing by and pick it up?" James said, smiling wryly.

'If James trusts this guy, what's stopping me from doing the same?' Mia thought to herself.

She smiled, grabbed his hand and walked towards the pickup point.

They walked for a short while, hand in hand, until they reached a light pole on a one-way street where a man dressed in a grey T-shirt, with a blue hooded jacket and baseball cap was standing with a sketchy looking garbage bag in his hands.

"Is this all of it?" James said inspecting the bag.

"Who is this? For fuck sake James! This isn't a bring-your-friends-to-work day!"

"Hey! Take it easy, she's in it with me." James said, holding his hand out to the man.

Mia struggled to get a good look at the mans face, but the baseball cap and the hood he had pulled over it from his jacket obstructed the view.

The man, realizing that Mia wasn't a threat, went on to say, "Yeah, it's quite a bit. Couldn't find a bag big enough to hold it. This'll have to do."

James took the bag from him and thanked him.

"You know the deal." the man said. "I'm in it for sixty percent, like the last time." He didn't give James a chance to say anything as he turned his back on the two of them and walked off.

"Who was that guy?" Mia asked.

James grabbed her by the waist and began walking towards the drop off point as he said, "The less you know, the better it is."

They walked, cocaine-filled-garbage-bag in hand, to the park, around the corner of which was a chain link fence that guarded what looked like a rundown building, graffiti running down the length of the old and beat up apartment complex.

"We pass this place every day, how come we never see it?" James said, taking in the sights.

"I hate to burst your bubble, but we were supposed to meet that guy here? Doesn't seem like he was interested after all." There was a bit of relief in Mia's voice. She didn't like the idea of dealing with this man to begin with. Everything about it seemed sketchy to her. The fact that he hadn't shown up yet was relieving her of the stress.

That relief however was short lived. The man was walking towards them with two bigger, more muscular, black men.

"Hey, we got what you asked for!" James said as they approached him.

"Yeah. Put it down in front of you and put your arms in the air." The man said

"Holy shit! They're cops!" Mia said, alarmed

A large man came up from behind Mia and grabbed her by the hair.

"Don't you fucking touch her!" James yelled as he punched the man on the nose, causing a steady stream of blood to pour down. The mans grip on Mia didn't loosen though.

James was caught and pushed into the chain link fence by the scrawny man and his three sidekicks.

"Okay, arrest me! Let her go! She has nothing to do with this!" James' cry for help was answered by insane laughter from the group of men.

"Look at this bitch, being a martyr all of a sudden." The man holding James' face to the chains said as he guffawed.

"We ain't cops punk!" One of the men behind him said

Mia was wincing in pain trying to break free from the hold she had been put in by the man who was clearly overpowering her.

"We're the sole suppliers for any kind of drugs in this neighborhood, and son, you just got your ass caught up in the wrong business. Now you're going to tell me where you got the cocaine from."

James tried to wrestle his arms free. "Let me loose and I'll tell you everything!"

The man let go of James' arm only to be punched in the jaw. The man was shaken a bit, lost his balance but his two men grabbed James. One mans knee was jabbed straight into his abdomen while the other punched him square on the mouth. James landed on his back, resting his head on the chain link fence, bleeding profusely from his mouth.

"I don't know the guys name." he said, coughing up blood. "I have an arrangement with him."

The scrawny man, who in James' mind had established himself as the leader of the pack, pulled out a knife from his pocket and held it close to Mia's cheek.

Mia was whimpering and screaming out James' name. The man behind her tightened his grasp and used one hand to cover her mouth.

"I'll talk! Just don't fucking hurt her okay!" James had tears running down his eyes and blood all over his face.

"I call a guy, I don't know his name. Tell him how much to get me, he gets a cut out of the sales!"

"How big a cut?" one of the bigger men asked.

"Sixty percent!" James said clutching his abdomen, pulling himself up with the support of the chain link fence.

"Did I tell you that you could stand up?" The scrawny man kicked James on his shin. "Sit the fuck down, fool!" James was knocked to the ground, in a world of pain.

"Is this all the blow he had?" the man asked.

James was in too much pain to talk. The men weren't sympathetic. They took turns stomping on him as Mia tried to kick, scream and claw her way free of her assailant.

"Knock the bitch out!" the man said not breaking his glance from a broken and battered James

One swift elbow to the back of the head and Mia was flat on the ground next to James

James, now crying in pain, yelled, "Yes! That's everything! Take it! Just leave us alone!"

The man picked up the garbage bag, ripped it open and poured the contents onto James and Mia's helpless bodies.

"Let that be a lesson to you!" the man said as he walked away.

James looked over at Mia lying unconscious on the ground next to him and cried, "I'm so sorry. I'm so sorr . . ." he blacked out, from the pain, next to her before he could finish.

James awoke just as dawn was about to break, to the sound of police sirens in the background.

Next to him, holding onto his shoulders was an awake and petrified Mia, covered in Cocaine, much like himself.

James gathered all the strength he could muster and pulled himself and Mia up.

"Let's get going. We don't want to get arrested tonight."

They stumbled to their apartment building; walked up the ill lit staircase to James' apartment.

Mia, now sober and brutally wounded, opened the door only to find it covered in plastic and filth with hideous looking walls that looked as though it was painted by all of hells demons.

Exactly the way they left it.

CHAPTER 9

BUSINESS TRIPS

'I'm broken. I can't bear to say anything to him, but I know it isn't his fault. I love him so much, but he's slipping away. We're slipping away. No! We're falling apart.' Mia thought.

———◆———

Mia hadn't said a word after the incident. She sat in the corner of the living room with her forehead resting on her knees. Un-bathed and unkempt with dried blood running down her nose. The only time she lifted her head up was when she heard police sirens outside the window. She'd assume the fetal position once again as soon as the sirens faded.

James had freshened up quite a bit since the assault. He had cleaned himself up, and managed to eliminate all the signs of the attack barring the bruising on his chest.

James moved closer to Mia and crawled up next to her. He tried to put his arm around her but she rejected his touch and pushed him away.

James didn't want to press her more than required so he pulled himself to his feet. The effort that it required was far greater than he had anticipated. He let out a grunt that went unnoticed by Mia, who was now sobbing uncontrollably.

James walked over to the couch in the living room and rolled up a joint with whatever little weed he had left over. He looked over at Mia who was starting to get to her feet. She picked herself up off the floor for the first time in hours and sat by James on the couch. She took the joint from his hand and lit it with a match that she found on the shaky table in front of her.

She inhaled deeply, and then slowly exhaled the smoke through her mouth. It pained her too much to breathe through her nose. *Must be broken,* she thought.

"How did we get here?" Mia asked James.

"We walked, well, I walked . . . I had to drag you for the most part." James said.

"No James! How did we end up here? All this pain and suffering. What do we have left to show for it?" Mia said, a tear rolling down her cheek, joint in hand.

James sat there and said nothing as the joint was passed to him.

He took a deep drag and rested his back on the couch.

"I don't know. I wish life came with a rewind button." he said.

"How far back should we rewind? Maybe I should've stayed with Bob. Maybe his impotency could be fixed. Maybe the two of us would've been happy—given a chance." She was beyond the point of thinking things to herself.

"What do you mean impotency? Doesn't he have two kids?" James asked, trying his hardest to not get on Mia's nerves by asking all the wrong questions.

"They weren't mine." She said as she took the joint back from James. "They were with his last wife, when he had no trouble getting it up and keeping it up. Apparently that divorce rattled him and made him less of a man."

"Worked out for me." James said as he looked around his apartment.

"What if I just made a big mistake?" Mia asked, the seriousness in her voice scared James but he knew that she had been through a lot and was just beginning to question her sanity.

"Too late to go back and change things." James said. "We weren't always miserable, were we?"

She put out the joint in the ashtray in front of her. "No." she said.

"We did have good times. We've just had a string of bad luck." he said while running his hand through his hair.

"Must be a pretty big ball of string." Mia said.

"It'll get better. It has to get better! How much worse could it get?" James said.

"It isn't going to get better if we stay put here in Rhode Island! There isn't anything left for us here James!" she said to him.

"Right, so we just pack up and leave? Where would we go?" he asked, playing along.

"Rouen!" Mia exclaimed. The thought of Rouen provoked a smile out of Mia. The first smile she genuinely felt deserved to be smiled in a long time.

"That port in France?" James asked confused. "You went there with your father, didn't you?"

"It's the most beautiful place I've ever been. I really think we have a shot of happiness there!" Mia was overjoyed with this discussion.

James didn't have the heart to break her from the hopes and dreams that Rouen carried for her but he didn't want her to have false hopes about the idea, so he asked; "How would we manage to move there? There's a question of immigration, of whether or not they'd let us live there and then the even greater question—money."

"We could make it! We were good at selling drugs before this happened! Why don't we . . ." She was cut short by a livid James who had now sprung up to his feet from his comfortable position on the couch and yelled, "Are you out of your mind? Have the last 24 hours been wiped off your memory? Those guys left us there to die with a garbage bag full of cocaine poured on us! For all we know the cops could be after us right now!"

Mia tried calming him down, "Hear me out!" she said, "If they're keeping an eye out for anyone, it's going to be a watchful one, but it'll be focused on you! They'd never think the puny girl would be pushing." Mia's eyes were determined and James could see that.

"I'm not letting you get caught up in that mess with those people! They're heartless and if they find out we're selling in their turf, they'll come after us and kill us!" James was trying to be the voice of reason.

"They want us not to sell in this neighborhood. They don't have bragging rights over the whole city, state or country!" Mia was kneeling on the couch now, as though some thoughts had put life back into her.

"I don't think I'm following. Please break it down for me." James asked, her proposal now seemed interesting merely because of the happiness that Mia was displaying. He loved Mia dearly; her happiness meant everything to him. So what if he had to risk his life for it?

Mia reached her arms up to find their grip firmly on James' shoulders, "Let's skip town. Head over to Massachusetts. We could sell some there, but we wouldn't want to attract too much heat, so we head over to New York after that!" Mia was exhilarated with her newfound business plan. James was beginning to come on board with the whole idea and that intrigued her more.

"We have 40% of everything from the last deal we made with you know who. We could use that to get more drugs and a car." James said.

"We can't just drive across the state with a car filled with drugs!" Mia exclaimed.

"Leave that to me. I know a guy." James said with a smirk.

Mia jumped up in excitement and kissed James on the lips, throwing herself onto him. James was taken by surprise and a strong pain was sent through his upper body.

"Ouch! Easy on the ribs" he yelped as he resumed kissing her.

———— •◆• ————

James woke up before the sun came out the following morning and walked to a nearby garage owned by his friend Josh.

Josh had a criminal record, but he had served his time and was out on parole a few years ago. His list of crimes included arson and grand theft auto.

Josh was leaning over a car, in his purple jumpsuit stained with grease with a cloth in his hand wiping the windshield; his scruffy blonde hair was tainted with the grease as well. James walked in through the front gate of the garage and Josh looked up at him and smiled.

"What brings you to my nape of the woods James?" Josh asked.

James reached over and hugged Josh. "I need a car." he said.

"Shit! Is this really happening? James has finally gathered the balls to talk to me after all these years. I really wish this meeting wasn't about business though." Josh said.

"Look man, about the arrest . . ." James began to say, but he was cut short.

"Naw man! It's cool! I'd have bailed too if the heat was on your ass. How were you to know the cops would show up before the car even got hotwired? You darted with the getaway car. I thought you were going to steal it; but you returned it safely in my garage." Josh wiped his brow and went on to say, "If you hadn't told my boys about my run in with the long arm of the law and told them to hide all the other cars by the time the cops showed up I'd never get out of the slammer. Good thinking kid!" Josh said as he patted James' back.

"Walk with me, let me show you what I got for you." Josh said as he walked through a door in the front of the garage, which led to a big hangar like storage unit for all his cars. Some stolen, some paid for in full and some, acquired. "What do you need?" Josh said pointing at the array of cars in his lot.

He had everything in that lot, a few beat up old muscle cars, some shiny low riders and even a few modern luxury sedans.

"I'm looking for something that won't garner too much attention." James said.

Josh laughed and went on to say, "Still up to your old tricks, huh?" He walked over to the far end of the lot and took James to an old Maroon Buick in pristine condition. Obviously refurbished.

"1977 Buick LeSabre. This one's a beauty. V6 Engine. Stole this one from Canada."

James looked up at Josh.

"Now I know what you're thinking. I repainted the car, I know a guy on the inside got me a new license and registration for this baby; just to be sure I changed the color. Trust me, the guy who used to own this car wouldn't recognize it if you drive right passed him." Josh said, reassuring James.

"Okay but I need some work done on it." James said.

"Just like the good old days." Josh laughed and said. "I knew that's what you wanted . . . so I showed you one that was already tricked out." Josh said as he began to rip open the seats of the car. Once the seat covers were removed, there were compartments made in between cushioning for hidden storage space. Even the mats under the seat came off with a layer of Velcro attaching it firmly to the ground to reveal hidden storage. "I used to push a ton of drugs across state borders in this car. Never been caught once. A Buick is an old mans car. They don't expect drug dealers to be driving around in one of these." He went on to say.

"Perfect!" James said, "How much would this set me back?"

"Don't be ridiculous man!" Josh handed James the keys. "Just bring her back to me in one piece. If you get arrested its going down on you buddy."

James nodded and hugged Josh. "Thanks! I owe you one!"

"You don't owe me my friend." Josh smiled, "We're even now."

James got into the car and drove off. He wanted nothing more than to take off with Mia but he had one more quick stop to make before Mia could see the car.

He drove up to the light post where he met up with his cocaine supplier the night before.

His dealer was standing there smoking a cigarette, no elaborate disguise this time. He was wearing a black wife-beater vest, exposing tattoos that ran down the length of his arm and ill fitted jeans. He had three backpacks, a bright orange one slung over his shoulders, a blue and black striped bag and a blood red one clutched firmly in either hand. His pale bearded face was visible.

"I heard you got beat up pretty bad?" the man asked.

James raised up his shirt and revealed the bruises. They'd started to become maroon-black from the light purple they were before.

"Ouch." The man said. "Look man, I'm not going to overlook the set back. So this time I'm going to take 75% of everything. Gotta make up for lost capital, you see?"

James nodded as he reached out for the backpacks. "You know I'm good for it." James said, reassuring the man that this setback was a one-time thing.

"I know man, but I'm a business man. I like my business like my dick. Always pointing up!" he chuckled. James was not amused by his humor or lack thereof; but he managed to force a smile nevertheless.

"Look this one's filled with hashish and weed and meth, my personal favorite is the meth though, cooked up a batch this week, pretty good stuff." The man was staring at the backpack as though he was analyzing the contents, but he never once opened them to peek inside.

James took that backpack and put it in the rear seat.

The man handed the blue and black backpack to James and James took it off his hands quickly.

The dealer went on to say, "This one's got all the fun stuff. Lots of different pills. Some E, some Smiley's some microdots. There's even some strictly prescription drugs in there, you know, for the up-market clientele."

James seemed please with this mans organization skills.

"Finally the goody bag." He said, as he held out the red bag, "This one's got your hallucinogenic drugs. There are so many mushrooms in here I'd watch out for frogs." he guffawed, still not amusing James. Sensing this he went on, "There's a bunch of acid in there and some salvia. You know, things that'll make a sane man think he's nuts."

James grabbed and tossed that bag in the backseat with the rest of them. "Got it! Weed, hash and meth in the orange bag, happy pills in the blue one and serious shit in the red one. Thanks a ton man! I knew you'd come through!" he said.

"Yeah, save the pleasantries. I want 75% this time! If you die selling 'em I'm going to rape your corpse!" the dealer said.

James made the strangest most confused face he could manage. He smiled and waved goodbye.

"75% James! Not a penny less!" he yelled as James drove off.

Of course James had no intention of paying him back. Soon him and Mia would be driving off to Boston, stopping along the way to make a few quick sales, then off to New York and finally to Rouen, where the only drugs they'd have to deal with were for their own amusement.

———— •◆• ————

The sun was peeking through the blinds into Mia's eyes. She tossed and turned her face away from the light, trying not to let this set back come in the way of the serenity she found in this nights sleep. That peace was short lived because a car outside was frantically blowing the horn. Mia was agitated and tossed her head under her pillow and held it down so as to cover her ears from the sound. But the honking was unbearable even through the padded cushion. Mia grunted and got off the bed to the window, she slid it open and yelled, "Shut the fuck up would ya!" without paying much attention to the car downstairs.

James got out of the driver seat and stood by the car. Mia held her hand up to her mouth and let out a scream of joy. "I'll be right down!" she yelled as she scrambled to put pants on and run down the hallway towards the car.

She exited the building and ran straight into James' arms.

"It's beautiful!" she said.

"I thought you'd like it." James replied.

"Are you kidding? I fucking love it!" she said.

She ran her hand along the hood of the car as she made her way to the passenger side door.

Once inside the car she looked around. There was an old CD player in the front, surprisingly it worked. The seat covers were made of cheap grey and black striped imitation leather that looked like the real deal to the untrained eye and the steering wheel was shiny. From the looks of things this car was spotless.

James sat in the driver seat. Mia hugged him and kissed his cheek.

"Shall we set off?" James asked.

"Right now?" Mia asked confused, "What about the clothes and the drugs?"

"Check and Check!" James said.

Mia just looked at him puzzled, James knew he had some explaining to do.

"Right now we're sitting on a shit load of drugs, our clothes are in bags in the trunk. We're good to go."

Mia jumped on the seat she was sitting on, "There are drugs in the seat?" She asked, elated.

"Yup! And check this out!" James said as he reached for the mat under her feet and pulled it up to reveal neatly stacked packets of different drugs. Mia got one good look at them and found herself in a state of awe. Her appreciation for James was at an all time new high. She quickly sealed up the mat and clapped her hands, "I'm so excited!" She said.

James pulled out two joints from his pocket and handed one to Mia.

"To business trips!" he said.

To business trips!

CHAPTER 10

GHOSTS

"Twenty, one, twenty two, twenty three, twenty four thousand dollars. And change." she counted.

"Since when is 876 dollars change?" he asked.

She smiled tossing the wads of money in the air and said, "We're in the big leagues now, babe! We're on fire!"

———— ◆ ————

James and Mia had made their way through the state of Massachusetts. They had become an even bigger success than they could imagine. They finished their stock of drugs a week into the state and no trouble from the police either. They had been pulled over for a few routine spot checks but neither of them was drunk at the time and the police had no reason to suspect enough drugs to kill a herd of elephants in the car seats. Even at the state crossings there were no real issues. They had gotten as far as Boston but their supply ran short. James eventually did return to his drug-dealing friend back in Rhode Island, he even paid of the 75% he had no intention of paying off in the first place and now had renegotiated the deal back down to 50%. That deal was now

10% less than the original agreement because he promised the sale to be quick and speedy. Why would anyone argue with a man that just sold more drugs in one week than anyone could in a lifetime?

James and Mia had an old motel off Hyde Park to call home for the short span that they had lived there. Run down motels had become a theme for this journey that they were undertaking. They could easily afford a plush hotel but they preferred to stick to their original idea.

The two of them wouldn't consume too much of their own products. Strictly doing only the little bits of weed or meth that they couldn't sell and the occasional strip of acid to celebrate a good day of sales.

They had become consumed with their work and that had become their high now. To them, they were at the peak of their lives. Raking in more money than they've ever been able to before, individually or together.

The two of them would work different streets at different times and never return to any street. They were careful not to linger around the same area for too long.

They had worked out a system. They worked through the statistics that people would much rather speak to women than men, so Mia would be the one that did the approaching. She was the pitcher, so to speak. James would be in an alleyway nearby overseeing the deal. When Mia would find out what the customer wanted, she'd return to James, who assumed the role of the Closer. He'd then take the drugs and make the final sale. This way if a cop ever had to bust anyone, it would be James. They'd have nothing to hold

Mia against, because she'd never actively have drugs on her. James had taught her to leave with the drugs and wait at the motel if the police ever showed up in the middle of a sale. Luckily, up until this point they had no run-ins with the law.

They'd successfully sold the second lot of drugs, and managed to cover everything from Brighton to Mission Hill to North End and West End.

It was time to head back for Rhode Island, increase their carrying capacity and head off to New York from there. The sales had been so good in Boston that they couldn't wait to up the ante.

———— • ◆ • ————

The two of them had managed to make over 50,000 dollars in the short time that they had been selling drugs across the country. Even after paying off the dealer the cut they owed him they had roughly thirty thousand to spare. The local newspapers in Massachusetts were beginning to talk about the increase in drug related arrests and they knew the time had come to leave the state for good. They were having a run of good luck and they didn't want to risk losing it all over greed so they headed back home.

They arrived in Rhode Island a few days later, stopping to make sales on the move and for rest. The only thing they needed to do there was to pick up more drugs from their drug dealing friend whose name they had now discovered was Chucky.

Chucky had come to terms with the fact that James had the ball in his court now. James had enough money to set up labs of his own and if that were to happen Chucky would be out of the equation. He knew he wasn't in a position to play hardball.

"So, the last batch of stuff flew off the racks, huh?" Chucky said, as he stood under his favorite light post wearing nothing but a pair of jeans and a beanie cap. "I got lots of new stuff for you to sell pal!"

"The last batch of meth you cooked for us came back with complaints." Mia said.

"Oh, hey, didn't see you there." Chucky said leaning down further as he spoke to Mia from across the driver side window.

"Cut the crap, bro!" James said, "Look we need better shit from you if we're going to keep working together. Our market is expanding and its expanding quick!" James said while toying with the steering wheel.

"Okay man, here you go!" he handed out six different colored bags to James; who didn't even wait for Chucky to explain the contents of the bags.

"Thanks Chucky, always lovely seeing you. Oh and by the way, new deal. 30% this time." James said while turning the ignition.

"30? Come on man, be fair! That just about covers the cost it took to make all that!" Chucky was clearly upset, you could tell by his body language.

"Take it or leave it Chuck." Mia said, curtly.

"Shit! I've got kids to feed!"

James hit the gas pedal and flew out of sight. Chucky was running along the side of the car, trying really hard to keep up yelling, "30%! Okay-okay! 30% is great! It's fucking fantastic!" James and

Mia were out of sight. Chucky stood there panting. "Fucking 30%! Ma's going to be pissed!" he said to himself.

"Could you stop by the house? There's something I want to pick up." Mia asked James. James nodded and headed towards home.

Mia walked up the stairs, and headed towards the apartment. Fumbled with the keys for a while then managed to open the door. The apartment was in exactly the same shape they left it. Painted tackily and covered in plastic. Mia fought with James about giving that place up a lot.

"You're paying rent for a place we don't even live in!" she said.

"I don't care! Other than you, that place is all I have!" he asserted.

She walked through the living room, passed a full-length mirror that was leaned up against the dresser in the hallway to the bedroom.

She took a few steps ahead and then walked back to the mirror.

She was stricken by grief when she looked at the reflection. She had been reduced to nothing but a bag of bones, her hair was graying a the roots and her teeth had become a shade of yellow that repulsed her. James and her had been so involved in the drugs that they didn't have time to look at each other. Mia grabbed on to her scalp in horror. She was howling in misery at the sight of her disfigured self. Her face was beginning to sag; the dark circles under her eyes made her look like a raccoon. She let go of her hair only to find strands of it, inches thick, being pulled out with the least bit of force applied. She was beginning to go bald. She could hardly recognize the face that was staring back at her, she was just a shell: a ghost of her former self.

She kicked the mirror, causing it to fall down flat on its face and shatter. She ran outside the apartment leaving the door opened and ran down to James.

She was crying frantically when James noticed her running out the apartment building. James got out of the car and hugged her and said, "What's wrong babe?"

"We have to stop James! We have to stop!" she said, tears flowing down her face.

CHAPTER 11

RHODE TO RECOVERY

"I can't go to a place as dear to me as Rouen looking like a hag! I can't do it!" Mia sobbed.

"If you want to go and throw everything we've worked for down the drain, go ahead and do it, don't expect me to play these fucking games with you!" he retorted

"You'll see James. When I'm better, you'll see that drugs aren't the answer to anything. I'm going to rid myself of these demons. I'll help you rid yours." she said, still sobbing

James was getting agitated, "Are you high right now? I don't see any demons."

———— •◆• ————

It had been a week since Mia had willingly enlisted herself into rehab. James had managed to do all the drugs that they had secured and then some, Mia took some money for the rehabilitation program, and getting help wasn't going to be cheap. While driving to pay the 30% he owed chucky he managed to ding the car in a few places. He'd probably blame the drugs or his emotional state for that but there was more to it than that. Between paying of debts and fixing the car, then returning it to Josh he had nearly no money left for himself. Whatever little he did save he managed to spend on more drugs.

James was beginning to lose his sanity, the plastic was being ripped off the furniture bit by bit, the walls weren't being repainted but redesigned completely. James had managed to rip out plaster using his nails off the dry wall. He wasn't doing so well without Mia. Even though Mia did try to contact him a few times through letters, he'd only read bits and pieces of them. The first letter she sent him he opened with great hope that she might be coming back to him. It read:

Dearest James,

They say I'm doing well so far. I told them all about the drugs and how I wished you could be here with me. I really wish you'd come visit me some day. It would bring me such joy to see your gorgeous smile one more time. I don't worry too much because I know how you feel about this place. You'd think with the amount of drugs we've done they'd put me in a padded cell somewhere, but really they're treating me alright. Every now and then I crave a fix but they tell me writing is therapeutic. Which is why I'm writing to you. I don't expect you to write back though. You were better with a brush than you ever were with a pen. Maybe send me a picture though? So I can remember how beautifully you paint?

They say I'll be home soon, so you don't have to worry about me for too much longer. I can't wait to hold you again, kiss you, breathe in your smell and just sit around and do nothing with you. I'm ridding myself of my demons. I'm going to come to rid you of yours too whether you like it or not, then . . . off to Rouen we go!

I think they're calling me to the mesh hall for supper now, the food here isn't great but at least the meals are warm. I hear there's pudding for dessert today, I know how much you love pudding, I'll sneak in an extra serving on your behalf.

Love,

Mia.

James was so enraged when he kept hearing Mia speak of 'demons' that he didn't know what to do with himself after reading her letters

All of them were about demons and ridding each other of them. James just wished she could see his side of the story. In his world there was absolutely nothing wrong with their lives. He loved her, she loved him and that was all there was to it. He was so mad at Mia for abandoning him that he had taken out the fury on himself. He hadn't left the apartment in weeks. He had eaten one too many magic mushrooms, smoked one too many joints and he blacked out.

The next morning when he woke up he found a letter sliding under the doorstep.

He walked up to it, of course, it was from Mia. No one else sent letters to him unless they were bills. This envelope couldn't be a bill though. Mia used rehab issued recycled brown paper envelopes to write to James. She'd always draw a squiggly heart on the top right corner and write James across the center, in cursive.

He tore the envelope open. The letter read:

> *Dearest James,*
>
> *Today they taught me that I was one step closer to freeing myself from the clutches of the demons.*

James didn't need to read further, he knew that this was one of those letters he didn't care enough to read. He wanted Mia back desperately. Her absence was sickening him.

He had fallen into a bit of a rut lately. Receive a letter from Mia, black out, and wake up only to find another letter from Mia, do some more drugs and then eventually sleep his life away.

The next few weeks brought more letters from Mia; each letter from her meant bad news for James. Each letter she sent was a day she could've gotten out of there and come see him, reunite herself with him. The promise of a new day was faded away completely for James when he'd see that brown paper envelope first thing in the morning.

This had gone on for days on end, days had become weeks. Weeks had become months. Nothing changed. There would be a new letter every day.

> *Dearest James,*
>
> *Life is good. The demons are leaving me . . .*

Then there were the occasional:

> *Dearest James,*
>
> *A few more days and I'll be home. Then we can go to Rouen . . .*

Nothing would break James' dedication to throwing his life away except seeing Mia again. He had decided that the next morning he would go over to rehab and lock himself up in there with Mia. He knew he could only be happy by her side. He was getting sick of staring at the pile of letters scattered all around his apartment. He was saddened by being alone, with no one to replace the void that Mia left.

Before he went to rehab, he had a lot of drugs to do. So he repeated his process. Mushrooms, methamphetamine, weed, acid, black out.

———•◆•———

The next morning Josh was knocking at the door.

"James!" he said while banging on the door. "Open up!" there was no response.

"James, the cops are on to you man for all those drugs you sold in Massachusetts! They tracked the car to me and asked me who I loaned it to. I tried to lie to them but they should be getting on to you soon man! If you're not home then great! Stay out! But if you are, please for your own sake, get the fuck out of town!" Josh walked away, afraid for James' wellbeing.

CHAPTER 12

ROAD TO RUIN

Knock knock knock . . .

The knocking had become a banging, but there was still no answer.

"I'm moving in, follow me." Agent Whitman said just before he banged James' apartment door off its hinges.

———— •◆• ————

There were four DEA agents and six armed policemen entering the apartment and searching the place. They found nothing but a pile of letters sprawled across the floor and motionless James sprawled across the living room couch.

"We got him." Said one agent into a walkie-talkie strapped around his vest.

James was clutching a letter it read:

Dearest James,

Tomorrow I'll be home. No more waiting, no more demons. We can finally begin our lives together. I hate the fact that you didn't write or send me that picture I wanted but I forgive you because there's no one I love more in this world. You are my world. I'm so happy that I'm coming home to you. I can't wait to kiss your lips again, I can't wait to feel your warmth and I can't wait to hold you in my arms through the cold nights. I've been so lonely James. Even while writing this, tears fall down my cheek. I sent you those letters everyday so that you'd never miss me. I hope you've been keeping well without me. I've been a wreck without you, but now I'm a wreck that doesn't need drugs. Not now. Not ever again.

You've always been the sole reason for my happiness. When I was married to Bob, you were there to get me through it, when I left him; it was you who I came home to. It may be the smallest apartment in the world, but it's my home. You make it that way. I could be in a hole in a wall, but if you were there that hole would become my home.

It's time for my final meal here at rehab! I am so excited about seeing you tomorrow! I wanted to surprise you but I wanted you to stay home for me and kiss me as I walk in the front door.

Love,

Mia.

PS: Rouen here we come! At long last . . . Rouen here we come.

The policeman held two fingers to James' neck. "Don't bother with the medical team. This one's already dead. Bring up the body bag." He shook his head sideways and said, "Drug overdose."

The medics were up within seconds, hauling James' body out of the apartment.

Rouen here we come . . . Rouen here we come . . .

ACKNOWLEDGEMENTS

Rhode To Rouen has been more of a journey for me than it was for my characters. Luckily for me I had some help along the way.

First off I'd like to thank my beta-testers: Natasha and Amanda for waiting on tenterhooks for me to finish writing the next chapter and for pointing out my grammatical indiscretions and of course the editorial team at Partridge India. I'd also like to thank everyone else that read the book in its embryo stages and gave me valuable feedback. That list, I'm afraid, is too long to pen out; but needless to say thank you all! All this would not be possible without help and encouragement from Mehirr who put me on to Partridge India, Hrishi K for helping me out in the early stages and of course, everyone else that wished me well along the way

Thanks to Farrina Gailey, Ann Minoza and the entire team at Partridge India for helping in making Rhode to Rouen everything that it is today.

And finally thanks to my parents: Anushka and Sunil that have put all their efforts into making me walk through life with rose-tinted glasses, who've supported me no matter what choices I made and who've made me everything that I am today. Thank you.